A DEATH IN THE PAVILION

by

Caroline Dunford

Magna Large Print Books
Long Preston, North Yorkshire,
BD23 4ND, England.

British Library Cataloguing in Publication Data.

A catalogue record of this book is
available from the British Library

ISBN 978-0-7505-4429-0

First published in Great Britain by Accent Press Ltd, 2014

Cover illustration by arrangement with Accent Press

The right of Caroline Dunford to be identified as the author of this
work has been asserted by her in accordance with the Copyright,
Designs and Patents Act, 1988

Published in Large Print 2017 by arrangement with
Accent Press

Magna Large Print is an imprint of Library Magna Books Ltd.

Printed and bound in Great Britain by
T.J. (International) Ltd., Cornwall, PL28 8RW

Chapter One

Relations

'Thwock! Thwock!'

Is there any sound more quintessentially British than the sound of leather on willow? The early autumn afternoons were beginning to get a slight chill, but it was refreshing and bracing. From my seat in the small pavilion I could see white-clothed figures running backwards and forewards across the small area of the pitch between the stumps. A distant cry floated to me on the wind; someone was out.

A long time ago before all my adventures began my little brother, Joe, had attempted to explain the vagaries of cricket to me. Although my Latin is good and my Greek passable, thanks to the efforts of my father, who believed in one exploring one's intelligence regardless of gender, I never did manage to get my head around cricket. As Joe explained the game, I remember thinking that it seemed more and more pointless and I didn't want to think that. I enjoy watching the game. It brings back memories of when my father was alive and he used to umpire the parish match each summer. All conflict between the parishioners, and there was much, was put aside as they ran trailing their well-worn bats behind them. Mr

Gregor, the exceedingly fat village grocer, would for once cheer on Mr Hainley the postman. All conflicts over which had the best beer, The Village Crown or The Empty Bottle, would be forgotten. It was a pure and peaceful time, punctuated by lemonade and thick-cut crusty sandwiches and cakes baked by the village women. Understanding the game would only have spoiled the moment.

Today I was far from my village home and my father had gone to his rest some two years hence after an unfortunate encounter with some mutton and onions. A demise so plebeian, I was unsure if my mother, the estranged daughter of an earl, had yet forgiven him. The bishop had whipped the rectory out from beneath our feet when the coffin was barely in the ground and tipped us out on the brink of destitution. Only an unexpected successful application for a maid's position at Stapleford Hall had saved me.

In the next two years came murder, intrigue, proposals from men who believed me to be no more than the working maid I claimed to be, and much heartache. I have written journals of all these adventures and the curious reader can learn much from perusing them. But suffice it to say at this time I am now companion to my once adversary, Richenda Stapleford, whose fiancé the late 'Baggy' Tipton was found hanging on the eve of their wedding. It is believed he killed himself after committing murder. In reality he was more than likely killed by Richenda's twin brother. Tipton was an unlovable soul. I suspect him of much. But all of this remains unproven. We live in an age when money and position trumps justice. In fact the first time I entered Stapleford Hall I encountered a murdered body, and shortly after the master of the house was also murdered. That time Bertram and I managed to get Richard arrested, but matters took their natural course and he became an MP.

He had once again won out over Tipton's death, but this time his sister had turned against him and just when it seemed Richard had made certain of my destitution, she rescued me and made me her companion. She did this not only to spite her brother, but because she needed a chaperone to take refuge at the estate of Hans Muller. Muller had been at the same school as Richard and Tipton. He has known the Staplefords a long time and is in some way connected with the prime rival bank to the Staplefords' in the city. When we had met at the court I had initially mistaken him for his cousin Frederick, which was quite unfair; for while there is a family resemblance, Frederick is older and much, much stouter. At the time I merely thought he had been on a weight-reducing diet.

Hans Muller has been nothing but kindness since we arrived and I have seen Richenda mellow under his influence. He is also a widower which lends almost as much attraction to him as the very lovely estate he had built in 1900. Now, eleven years on, the estate is in its prime. The gardens delightful, the special tower built for ladies' afternoon tea splendid, the marble dairy a masterpiece of modernity, and the staff copious. The main house is respectably large without being brash, but has the requisite room for balls and banquets, which remain modestly (and very Britishly) shuttered at all times when not in use. The only handicap Muller suffers from, apart from his Christian name, which he never uses, is his mother. She is, to put it kindly, eccentric. His German father has had the decency to depart this mortal coil long before the current difficulties with Germany, but his mother remains an embarrassment. Unfortunately for Muller, he clearly loves his mother very much and thus cannot take a typical Stapleford way out of the situation and dispose of her.

Even the seasons seem to be kinder here. Though the leaves are beginning to change, the exotic flower known as Angel's Trumpet still flowers and curls around the pavilion. The paint is beginning to crack on the wood and the resident gardener will be seriously neglecting his duty if this is not seen to before the cold weather sets in. The pavilion is also beset with cobwebs and spiders; while this holds no fear for someone who has had a little brother like Joe, I do wonder why the maids do not clean it. The view over the cricket ground and out towards the south lawn induces a feeling of calm and relaxation such as I have not known for the past two years. It is a lovely spot, so it confuses me why I am the only one who takes advantage of it. Even the cricketers themselves do not use it, but prefer to bring a picnic to the side of the pitch for their refreshment. Still, on the positive side, it means that when I sit here, reflecting on both the past and my uncertain future, no one disturbs me. Until today.

'Miss! Miss!' Lucy, one of the housemaids erupts onto the pavilion floor. She is breathless and her cap is askew. Her pretty young face is flushed pink and curly tendrils of blonde hair are escaping their pins. She is normally the neatest and most precise of the maids. 'Whatever is the matter?' I asked, starting to my feet. 'Is Miss Richenda ill?'

I confess the tone of worry in my voice is as much for my own position as for Richenda. It is hard to love an employer who once locked you in a cupboard.

'I've been looking for you everywhere,' panted Lucy.

I frowned. 'I would have thought it was quite likely I would be out watching the cricket.'

'I've been all over the gardens,' replied Lucy, sounding a little stung. 'It never occurred to me you would be here.'

'In the cricket pavilion? Watching the cricket?'

'No one comes here,' said Lucy. 'Not after what happened to the Mistress.'

'What–' I began, but Lucy was not to be interrupted this time.

'Miss Richenda wants you now in the morning room. She is entertaining a Lady.' The last word was said with an undoubted capital L. Muller may be a successful banker and he may be fortunate enough to mix with them in society, but as yet he has been unable to bring many home. Obviously the household was in a fluster over this arrival. My curiosity was piqued.

'Lead on,' I said to Lucy. 'But at a reasonable pace. I do not wish to arrive flushed.'

'Miss Richenda has been asking for you this past half hour!'

I gave Lucy the look I had learned when I had taken over from Mrs Wilson in my short-lived tenure as housekeeper at Stapleford Hall, and she capitulated. 'This way, Miss,' she said and set off at a more moderate pace. I could see her fingers flexing with frustration. Richenda had been among them barely a month, but the staff, if not Muller, already knew her temper.

But when Lucy finally opened the door to the morning room I was faced with a Richenda who was almost purring.

She rose as I entered (in itself remarkable), a warm smile of greeting on her face. I knew her well enough to notice this smile did not reach her eyes. 'My dear Euphemia,' she cried. 'Such a delight. The daughter of the Earl of ------- has come to morning coffee!'

And with that she introduced me to a lady, who having been obscured by the opening door, only now came into view.

My mother.

Chapter Two

Social Niceties

To give her credit my mother responded impeccably. She did of course know I was in service and even that I was using a false name. However, she had every reason to believe that I was miles away serving as a housekeeper at Stapleford Hall.

Considering the turmoils of my recent times I had decided it was best to be an infrequent correspondent.

'Euphemia,' said my mother coming forward and giving her hand, 'what a lovely name. I have a daughter of that name, but I am sad to say she has turned out a little wild.'

'A fault I am sure you will correct,' said Richenda with a simper, 'she must be very young and breeding will out.'

'You would think so,' said my mother, looking me directly in the eye.

'How charming to meet you,' I said. 'I did not know Mr Muller had such distinguished neighbours. Is it too much to hope your daughter will also be joining us?'

My mother, no matter how strict, is not without humour and I saw a distinct twinkle in her eye. 'We are very close,' she said. Then turning to Richenda she said, 'It is almost as if she is with me right now.'

I felt this was taking things too close to the wind and interrupted. 'Are you a resident of this parish?' The last I had heard she had been living some considerable distance away in a rented cottage, earning extra money by giving piano lessons. I felt for her pupils.

'I am visiting an old friend of my husband's. The local vicar, Mr Chorley. I have brought my young son with me. His Greek has finally overtaken mine and I must ready him for school shortly.' She gave a little laugh. 'Not that he agrees. Given the chance he would run wild.' She eyed me carefully. 'In fact, I believe the gardener is currently showing him the grounds.'

I breathed an inward sigh of relief. I was indeed lucky that Joe and his love of cricket had not brought him to my side. He too knew of my subterfuge, but the reliability of a young boy who would swap his mother's best teapot for an excellent conker is not something in which one wishes to place one's safety.

'Anyway,' said my mother briskly, 'this has been a most delightful morning, Lady Stapleford. I hope we may soon have the pleasure of your company at the rectory, if you will condescend to visit. Mr Chorley has bid me make myself at home. He is a bachelor and I believe somewhat relieved to have a lady in residence, who can manage his staff and his menus. He is the younger son of the Duke of -------, you know. He has been given the title of canon now, and his rectory is unusually large, but I believe the family is most disappointed he never made it to be a bishop.'

Richenda's eyes gleamed at being told such society gossip. In fact, any more and I was certain she would start to drool. The Staplefords are new money and their title only as old as her late father. All of them are desperate to move into High Society. Personally I cannot think of anything worse.

'I believe Mr Muller's late wife was the rector – I mean canon's sister?' asked Richenda, trying to join in the game.

'I expect that was the previous incumbent of the post,' answered my mother without batting an eyelid. 'I have not had the pleasure of meeting Mr Muller, but I understand he is foreign.'

14

Richenda inhaled sharply, but maintained a calm facade. 'I assure you, my lady, he is quite the English gentleman.'

'Excellent,' said my mother, 'that must be so much more comfortable.' Than what she didn't say. 'And now,' continued my mother, 'I must collect my son. I believe the last I saw him the gardener had taken him under his wing. Do give my regards to Mr Muller's mother. I was sorry she was not well enough to join us.' It was clear from my mother's face this was a patent lie, but Richenda swallowed it with good grace.

'If you will wait a moment, my lady, I will speak with the housekeeper and she can arrange to have your son brought to us.'

My mother nodded graciously and sat once more. Richenda hurried out the door. 'Goodness,' said my mother, 'they must have four hundred servants here if they have a dozen and she leaves the room to find one!'

'Good morning, Mother,' I said. 'Did you know I was here?' I bent over and dutifully pecked my mother on the cheek.

'I had heard there was a Stapleford staying with the Mullers and as it seemed perfectly unsuitable I thought there was a good chance I would find you here.'

One point to Mother.

'And you are staying with an old friend of Father's. A bachelor friend.'

My mother nodded as she accepted the riposte. 'I am not yet beyond marriageable age, Euphemia. It would answer many of our problems.'

'To another vicar?'

'A canon,' corrected my mother, 'but although this one is the son of a duke, he is a younger son, not only without money, but also without ambition. I fear it is not to be thought of.'

'Mother, do you even care for him?'

'I care for Little Joe and you,' said my mother.

'I would not have you wed a man you did not like for my sake and I doubt Joe would either,' I said.

My mother sighed. 'It is not coming into question now. Personally I am unhappy at having a daughter in service. Very unhappy.'

'No one knows of our connection.'

'At least you are now a companion. Even if your employer is far below your own social station.'

'Earlier this year I became engaged to the son of a greengrocer,' I said.

My mother went white. 'Euphemia,' she shrieked.

'Sadly,' I continued, 'I have been so well brought up to a station I cannot inhabit that he jilted me as he felt he could never be good enough for me.'

My mother's breathing slowed and she patted herself on the chest. 'A man of sense.'

'A good man,' I said bitterly. 'A man my father would have liked.'

'Even Bertram Stapleford would be better than that!'

'I see you have been doing your research,' I said. We were now eyeing each other with hostility tempered with inbred affection.

'We must hope Little Joe doesn't let your secret – how do these people say it – out of the bag?' said my mother.

'You didn't warn him I might be here?' I gasped in horror just as the door opened.

My little brother bounced into the room. He was considerably less little than the last time I had seen him. It was clear he would in a very short space of time be towering over my mother's petite 4'11" frame. His hair was curly as ever and his features still retained their childish (and completely misleading) cherubic nature. 'Mater!' he cried, 'Do you know they found a body in the pavilion!'

I felt the world darken around me. I barely suppressed a cry of 'Oh no, not again,' as I sank into an over-stuffed chair. My legs shook and my heart appeared to be attempting to break out of my ribs.

Incredibly, Richenda, entering behind, tittered. 'How do boys discover these things?' she said with a conspiratorial smile at my mother.

'A body of what or whom?' said my mother, showing remarkable fortitude.

'Mrs Muller,' said Little Joe, who still had not noticed my presence. 'The gardener told me.'

'Oh he really shouldn't have,' said Richenda. 'I do apologise.'

'Mrs Muller?' I said weakly.

Richenda went off into a peal of laughter. 'Oh. Euphemia, your face!' Then she pulled herself together. She had undoubtedly caught sight of my mother's face. 'Of course, it is not a laughing matter, but what a misunderstanding. And it is so long ago.'

'I take it we are discussing the late wife of Mr Muller, not his mother,' said my mother.

Richenda nodded. 'Yes, she was found dead in the pavilion three years ago I believe. A weak

17

heart. Quite terrible for Muller of course, but so long ago now.'

My mother made a pithy response, but Little Joe and I had now locked eyes. I shook my head very slightly. In response my brother's eyes grew round as saucers. My mother now turned her attention to him and started scolding him for repeating such a tale. The room seemed over-full of people and oppressively hot. I was seriously considering fainting when the door opened once more and Mrs Philomena Muller, mother of the master of the estate, entered. 'Guests we are having?' she enquired of Richenda loudly. 'Introduced I must be!'

'My dear, Philomena,' said Richenda hurrying forward, 'I understood you to be resting or I would...'

Mrs Muller had not closed the door behind her and I made use of the opportunity to exit. Sliding out of my seat and away from the uproar.

What I needed, I told myself, was a nice cup of tea. As a companion of Richenda's I was meant to be in her company as much of the time as possible. However, Mrs Muller being in residence and having taken to Richenda, I had quietly been awarded my own small sitting room where I could indulge in outlandish and unladylike habits like reading. I made my way there now and rang the bell.

A companion's lot is not a happy one. We don't quite fit into the social hierarchy. Richenda had not let it be known I was once a maid and housekeeper and though Muller knew he had said nothing. Therefore the staff, all four hundred-odd of them, had been assessing me over the last few weeks. As far as I knew they had yet to make up their minds. I, on the other hand, had determined my role from the moment we drew up on the impressive and very new drive. Country people don't like new money and new ways. I felt certain Muller would be disliked, but in fact not one of the staff had a bad word to say about him. He had designed his estate with complete efficiency. He paid his staff a reasonable salary for a country estate. He was known to be fair in all disputes and never to have a cross word in the normal way of things. He was described by all as a charming gentleman and no reference was made to his foreign-ness. He had a very loyal staff. The role he had undoubtedly designed for his mother was very clever. She was the one who threw temper tantrums, scolded maids who failed in their duty, and gave orders for anything that could be considered remotely out of the ordinary. She was feared, but respected because of the general appreciation of Muller. I had no doubt it had all been cleverly arranged.

Richenda did not know how to behave in a large estate and often made mistakes. She was not above gossiping with the maids, as she had done with my good friend Merry at Stapleford Hall. The difference of course was that she and Merry had almost grown up side by side. The staff here were contemptuous of her. Her recent defence of Muller to my mother gave weight to my growing suspicion that she was contemplating him as a husband. If he should offer I had no doubt he would also do this charmingly. His staff, however, would be hell to tame.

For my part I treated all the staff politely, never

asked for anything to excess, but I was careful never to do anything that might lower my position. Which was why I was ringing for tea rather than going to the kitchen to ask for some – something Richenda had done on our first week here. I despaired of her.

Lucy popped her head around the door. 'Anything I can get you, Miss St John?' she asked.

'Oh, Lucy, I could really do with a nice cup of tea, please.'

'Of course,' said Lucy, entering rather than leaving. 'It all got a bit heated in the morning room from what I heard.'

I had the choice now of engaging in gossip or snubbing her. A companion who gossips is highly prized by a household staff, but also loses respect from her lack of loyalty. A companion who snubs the staff is liable to be thought above herself and cold tea will be the least of her contrived inconveniences. I tried a lateral approach.

'I quite misunderstood the young boy and thought he had found a body in the pavilion,' I said, striking a happy balance between truth and a suitably shocking topic.

'Oooh,' said Lucy and made to sit down on one of the chairs. A raised eyebrow halted her progress.

'I believe he had heard the tale from the gardener.'

'Mr Bennie. He was the one that found the body. It's coming up to the third anniversary. Must have been on his mind.'

'She had a weak heart,' I said invitingly.

'Well, that's what the doctor said, but if she had she'd kept it very quiet. Mind you, she wasn't one

20

of these ladies that like to complain, like.' Unlike some I could mention, hovering on the air between us. I was going to have to have a word with Richenda. I gave a slight nod of acknowledgement, but Lucy took it as encouragement. 'Sweet, she was. Much younger than Mr Muller, but you know how he is. He could charm the birds out of the trees and she was completely bowled over by him. Why when he was in the room she had no eyes for anyone or anything else. Always together they were. Why even when he went up to town for business he took her with him. Stayed at the poshest hotels. And her no more than a vicar's sister. Course she were lovely like, to look at. But no children. That were the real tragedy. Miscarried five and Mrs Muller distraught each time.'

'How sad,' I said.

'Course, he will have to marry again, some time,' said Lucy. 'We're all hoping he'll pick a real lady this time. With his charm and wealth he should be able to look as high as he likes for a bride.' This was said with a challenging air.

'And I think a teacake too,' I said, bringing our conversation to an end.

'Of course,' said Lucy, who knew the rules of the game all too well. 'Milk or lemon?'

'Oh, I think lemon at this time of day, don't you?' Lucy nodded approvingly and left.

I was left pondering the late Mr Muller's marriage. Had it been love's young dream or was it a description of a young woman overbearingly controlled by an older husband; her eyes following him everywhere not out of love, but fear?

21

Chapter Three

A Charming Gentleman

That very evening I had cause to rethink my speculations. Unexpectedly Muller arrived back from town. The pff-futt of his motor cut through the late afternoon as I sat with Richenda as she did her best to embroider a cushion. I can only say it was fortunate that the thread she was using was red.

He entered the sitting room not half an hour after we had heard his arrival. He was neatly dressed and his hair impeccably combed. Any smuts from the road had been totally removed, but he had not yet changed for dinner.

He came across the room, his hands out-stretched towards Richenda. 'My dear Richenda, are you well? I left the city as soon as I heard.'

I raised a puzzled eyebrow. My mother might have been known to make waves in social circles in her youth, but it seemed unlikely that even she could have upset the workings of the city. Besides, she would have considered even knowing about such matters far too vulgar.

Richenda happily took his hands. Muller was not prone to displays of such affection. I wondered if he would regret his impulsiveness when he found his palms and cuffs covered with pinpricks of blood. Richenda really was an extraordinarily bad needlewoman. Worse than myself, and my mother would tell you that is no mean feat.

Muller held the embrace and searched her eyes. 'You are being so brave,' he said. Richenda inflated before my gaze with pride. However, I could see she had no idea what he was talking about, but was simply basking in the moment.

'Mr Muller,' I interrupted, shocking the gentleman into realising he had been holding her hands too long. He dropped them at once and turned to face me. Richenda did an excellent impression of a basilisk at me.

'My dear Miss St John, at your post by our dear friend's side,' he said. 'I did not see you sitting in that corner, but I should have known you would be on hand at this difficult time.'

'Mr Muller, I fear you have the advantage of us. Neither Richenda nor I know to what you are referring?'

Mr Muller started, somewhat over-dramatically I felt, and said, 'It is possible I have beaten him here? I drove like the wind, but I was sure he would reach here before me.'

I began to feel that I had stumbled into a melodramatic gothic novel, but Richenda appeared to be enjoying the experience. She clasped her hands to her chest and asked in a quivering tone, 'Who is coming, Mr Muller?'

It was at this tender moment I became sure that Muller and Richenda had set their sights on each other. Richenda's betrothed was not long dead, but they had not made it to the altar, so a period of mourning was not set in societal stone. Muller I had suspected of eyeing Richenda's shares in the Stapleford bank, but she wasn't high society, or even that attractive if I am painfully honest, and while he was not more than ten years older than her he was not only foreign but no one could have denied his hair was thinning.

I need not tell you having a bald husband, unless he is of the highest standing, is something of a social faux pas in this age of moustaches and side whiskers.

The two of them appeared to be still locked in their tableaux. Both had forgotten it was almost time to dress for dinner. 'Who is coming?' I asked as calmly as I could.

Muller used the urgency of his news to again clasp Richenda's hands through he turned to respond to me. 'Richard Stapleford has sent his agent to bring Richenda home.'

Thoughts of a rough man in tweed with a cosh passed through my head. 'What agent?' asked Richenda.

'He has hired a new factotum to help him manage his estates now he has bought up the Bellfield property. A London man.'

'Then he is probably lost down some country lane,' I suggested. 'Your estate, Mr Muller, is not the easiest to find and I doubt a man with a London accent would get much help from the local people.'

Muller beamed. 'What an excellent thought, Miss St John. Why I believe we can relax and dress for dinner. Richenda need have no fear that she will be compelled to do or go anywhere she does not wish while I am here.'

The look Richenda gave him would have made

Little Joe lose his luncheon on the spot. I fled before my appetite could be completely eroded.

I am not totally hard-hearted and I certainly do not wish Richenda ill, but should she marry Muller I would again be in a vulnerable position. I had to continue to earn a wage to support my mother and brother or my mother would indeed have to marry the canon regardless of his lack of ambition.

As the master of the house had returned, dinner became enlarged by a course. Mrs Muller preferred soup, fish, and a cheese plate when her son was away, but Richenda's moanings about feeling faint had ensured we received soup, fish, and a proper dessert. This evening included a meat course. As Muller carved the roasted joint Richenda appeared to be in seventh heaven, but whether this was due to the extra course or her budding swain was hard to tell.

In fact it was Mrs Muller who appeared the most out of sorts. Normally she was delighted to see her son home.

'Are you sure you have not left things undone, Liebling?' she asked over the tomato and pepper soup.

'Nothing urgent is demanding my attention,' her son assured her.

'I am sure you always said that this time of year was most demanding with people away from the city in hotter climes.' That Mrs Muller was now speaking in the most correct English did not escape my attention.

Muller smiled. 'It is true that sometimes deals can be achieved while other competitors are sunning themselves, but I have some excellent staff who will take care of my interests.'

Dover sole, accompanied by asparagus spears, and the tiniest potatoes appeared next. No one mentioned the order of the courses. The footman had barely deboned my fish before Mrs Muller suddenly said, 'I think family should be together, do you not, Miss St John?'

The eye on my fish looked up at me pityingly. 'I rather think it depends on the family,' I said awkwardly. 'For example, no one could doubt that you and your son live most happily together, but for some mothers and their adult children it is not so easy.'

'My mother is the easiest woman to live with,' said Muller. 'She only wants my happiness and success. She has quite spoilt me for other women.'

'Not, I would hope,' said his mother, 'for the right Lady.' There was considerable emphasis on the last word.

'Of course,' said Richenda, 'your mother would want nothing but the best for you. She would want you to marry the woman you loved.' And she cast him such a glowing look I wondered if she had any idea how transparent she was being.

Muller merely smiled and turned his attention to his fish. Richenda and Philomena Muller sized each other up across the table. I concentrated on my plate.

I did my best to appear totally ignorant of the battles that were being waged with what the participants charmingly believed was subtlety over the courses. My head was buzzing with ideas. Mrs Muller had been the most doting of hostesses towards Richenda and myself until tonight. Could it be that she had not foreseen her son might become enamoured of his guest? Before tonight I could have sworn she would have had no objection to Richenda becoming her daughter-in-law. I knew her to be an intelligent woman and despite what his loyal servants might aspire towards, I had been certain she knew how high he could aim for a bride and that Richenda with her shares and comparative youth was no bad bargain. But tonight the first time the pair had effectively acknowledged the possibility of a future together she had taken grave offence.

And why was Muller moving towards a declaration now? I felt he had given Richenda refuge partly to annoy Richard and also because I think he had suspected more than most what Richard was capable of doing.

No doubt something was indeed happening in the city and Richenda's shares had become important. Richard's decision to send an agent showed an unusual amount of sense. Richenda would have had no qualms about sending her twin brother packing, but even she knew an agent would be a source of information about what was happening back at Stapleford Hall, an estate the three siblings all held an inordinate affection for despite its continued series of murderous calamities. Muller, of course, also wanted to question the agent. Though he would be seeking business information. I remained conflicted as to whether he aimed to be Richenda's saviour or was merely capitalising on the opportunity. A man so charming must have many secrets to hide.

Mrs Muller stood signalling it was time for the ladies to retire. 'Mother, please don't go,' said Muller.

'But we should do things properly, Hans. You are a country gentleman now.'

Muller's eyebrows shot up momentarily. The estate had been under his command for ten years. 'I would very much like to you stay, Mother, as I have a project to suggest. Besides I do not care enough for port to drink it alone.'

Mrs Muller hesitated. If she defied her son it would be the first time I had seen it. Muller got up and held out her chair for her. She sat.

'I have been thinking,' he said, 'that it is time for us to revive the autumn ball.'

Richenda's face lit up. 'Oh, how very exciting,' she said. 'You have a ballroom here, do you not?'

Of course she knew he did. The first time he had headed up to town and Mrs Muller had taken her afternoon rest, Richenda had taken the opportunity to explore the state rooms and look under all the dust covers.

'It is only three years,' said Mrs Muller. 'People may feel it is inappropriate.'

Muller bowed his head. Then looked at Richenda. 'It was the day after our autumn ball, three years ago, that my late wife died. I stopped the tradition to honour her.'

'Of course,' said Richenda, 'I quite understand.' One of her hands clenched her glass stem so tightly I feared for it. 'But...' she said and let the word hang in the air.

'But,' continued Muller for her, 'No man – or woman – is expected to mourn for ever. However exceptional their spouse.'

Mrs Muller muttered something about Queen Victoria and we all pretended not to hear.

'I met my wife in autumn, but seven years earlier in a previous autumn I laid the foundations of this estate. It is my intention to hold the ball to celebrate the ten-year anniversary of the house. I will not be making it, this year, a – er – London society ball. That would seem distasteful, but I should like to invite the local gentry and some of my oldest friends. Then later when we have let it known our doors are open once more perhaps we will tackle a bigger event.'

A war of expressions raged across Mrs Muller's face. The thought of London society eventually returning to the house and presumably the advent of eligible young ladies for her liebling was temptingly delicious.

'I thought perhaps while Richenda was here she could help you with all the details, Mama. Take much of the work from you.' He turned to face Richenda. 'If it is not impudent to ask?'

'Oh, I would love to do it,' said Richenda eagerly. 'Euphemia has acted as my brother's secretary before and could do some little tasks.'

I knew this to mean she would expect me to do everything for her.

'Ah, yes indeed, Miss St John,' said Mrs Muller. 'It would be an honour to work with you.' I could only stare at her. Words failed me completely. Until now she had largely ignored me. Richenda bristled at the slight and Muller gazed into the middle distance studiously ignoring the chaos he had wrought among us women.

It was perhaps fortunate for all of us that at this time the butler appeared and sidled up to Muller to whisper in his ear.

Muller sighed. 'It appears your brother's man, Gilbert Barker, has indeed arrived,' he said. 'He is asking to speak with Miss St John.'

Chapter Four

No Dead Bodies

Three pairs of eyes looked at me with varying levels of suspicion. Muller nodded slightly and I rose. Richenda began to protest as I exited the room. On the short walk to meet this stranger, I can put it no other way than to say a dark prescience began to overtake me to the extent that I would not have been surprised to find him stretched out on the fine Persian rug with his throat cut. Later, when I came to know Gilbert Barker, I would think it was a very great shame this did not happen.

The ubiquitous Lucy showed me to the library. She left me at the door. My fingertips trembled against the cold metal of the door handle. I gave myself a mental shake. I told myself that this was only words. People were behaving oddly tonight, but considering how volatile the Staplefords had been over the years this situation should not be rattling me as much as it was. I took a deep breath and opened the door.

Mr Gilbert Barker stood there very much alive. He was tall and thin with short, curly ginger hair. He wore a suit of the best cut but it sat uneasily on him. An unflattering five o'clock shadow framed a thin, pinched face set with dark eyes. His age could have been anywhere between thirty and forty-five. He had what can only be described as a lived-in face.

'Euphemia,' he said and gestured to a seat. 'I had the maid bring a decanter and glasses. I think we are both going to need some whisky.'

'I do not believe we have been introduced, sir.'

'Oh, no need to call me sir, Euphemia. After all you don't exactly work for Sir Richard any more. Barker will do.'

'And Miss St John will do for me,' I replied making no move towards the indicated seat. Barker walked across and sat down in one of the seats. He poured two glasses of whisky, one much larger than the other, which he placed in front of himself. 'Do at least close the door behind you, Euphemia. There is a draught.'

'I will happily do so from the other side,' I said, turning to go.

'Miss St John, you have secrets. Ones I think you do not care to share.'

I pushed the door hard closed behind me, took my seat, and demanded, 'What secrets?'

Barker shrugged. 'I have no idea, but obviously ones you don't want shared with your current employer. I shall have to ask Stapleford to fill me in. And make no doubt he will. I am his right hand.'

Internally I let out a great sigh of relief. He knew nothing. But since I was here I might as well get the interview over and done with. 'What do you want?' I asked.

Barker pushed the smaller glass towards me. I pushed it back. He picked it up and poured it into his own glass. 'I hate waste,' he said.

I did not repeat my question, but waited. Obviously a little of Fitzroy had rubbed off on me. However, while I had never had any doubts that the spy Fitzroy would shoot me if he had to – with I hoped a soupçon of regret, I had never felt that physical violence hovered about him as it did with Barker.

Barker took a sip of his whisky. He gave me a thin smile. 'I can say one thing for this German, he knows his whisky. But then foreigners are often more accurate on these things than real gentlemen. It's all to do with keeping up the pretence, isn't it, Euphemia?'

It hovered on my tongue to tell him that he should know. Clothes do not maketh the man and all that, but I refused to allow myself to be baited and sat quietly with my hands folded in my lap.

'If Sir Richard had not briefed me fully on you and your services to the family,' said Barker, 'I might take you for the insipid companion of moderate intelligence that you are pretending to be, but we both know that is far from the truth.'

Words, I told myself, it is merely words. 'Your empty threats aren't even fully formed,' I said.

Barker gave a crack of laughter. 'Oh, we haven't got to the threats yet. I am here to open up communications between Sir Richard and his beloved sister once more. Sir Richard is mindful that she has no claim on the Mullers and that her prolonged residence here is beginning to cause talk. And we both know how dangerous talk can be, don't we Euphemia? Why it can even land innocent men in jail.'

'I don't believe Sir Richard was ever tried, so technically we cannot say if he was guilty.' I paused. 'Or not,' I added.

Barker's eyes narrowed. I knew I was over-stepping the mark, but much as I have disliked Richenda in the past I felt a rather surprising desire to protect her from her brother. One's training as a vicar's daughter is always inescapable.

'I see you believe in straight talking,' said Barker, 'so do I. It makes things much easier. You and I Euphemia are not unlike. We both work for difficult masters and we both make our way in the world determined by the success of these masters. Richenda has little social status. The suspicious death of her father, compounded with her age, her fondness for the suffragettes and fallen women and not least her undeniable facial similarity to a horse all stand against her. Now she is again linked with death as her almost husband kills himself, embarrassing his relations and proving himself to be of unsavoury character. All she has is some money and a few shares in the family bank. Nothing else stands in her favour. I believe you know all too well her unappealing character. Shut you in a wardrobe, didn't she?'

'At the time she believed she had to do so to support her twin,' I said with more forgiveness than I had ever felt before.

Barker jumped on this. 'And this time her twin wants to stand by her. Sir Richard is becoming more prominent in parliament, his business is progressing and he may soon be entering into a very successful engagement. He can rescue his sister from her downward spiral into obscurity and possibly even attempt to find her a husband in a year or two when her social disgrace has abated.'

'Social disgrace!' I cried, jumping to my feet, 'I'd like to see you say that to her face! Richenda has done nothing wrong except give her heart unwisely.'

'I have no intention of saying it to her face,' said Barker. 'That is why I am talking to you. You need to get Richenda to see that it is in her best interests to return home.'

'But I don't see that it is,' I said coldly. 'I have known Sir Richard for a little time now and, if we are speaking plainly, I have never seen him do anything for his sister's sake or for any other sake than his own.' I remained standing. Barker lounged back at this ease. His entire attitude was an insult, but still I stayed. I knew a threat was coming and it would be real whether or not I chose to hear it.

'Euphemia, such a display of affection for someone who would not grieve for a moment if you fell and broke your neck! She really isn't worth your defence. Her brother wants her back. Advise her of this. Persuade her of the advantages of this. Get her out of the house of this ruddy German and back where she belongs.'

'Where she belongs or where her shares belong?'

Barker shrugged. 'It doesn't matter to you. What matters is if you stand against Sir Richard on this you will find him a formidable enemy.'

'You overestimate my influence on Richenda,' I

said flatly.

'For your sake, let us hope I do not,' said Barker and he rose. 'Sir Richard will be paying his compliments in person shortly. Ensure his sister receives him well. Or it will go badly for both of you.'

'An empty threat?'

Barker jammed his hat back on his head. 'Oh, you know only too well what Sir Richard is capable of doing should he not get his own way.' Despite my intention to stand up to this jumped-up little man a shiver ran down my spine. This was as close to a death threat as he could have uttered.

He made his way to the door, brushing past me rudely. He stood with his hand on the door handle for a moment as if deciding whether or not to speak. Then he turned back towards me one last time. 'Besides, you do know Muller murdered his first wife, don't you?'

Chapter Five

Attic Adventure

'So what did he want?' fired Richenda the moment I returned to the dining-room.

'Your brother sends his regards and would like you to come home,' I said simply.

Muller raised one elegant eyebrow. 'I suspect you are giving us the shortened version?'

Richenda got to her feet. 'Did he threaten you?' she demanded.

'To be honest,' I said taking my seat and attempting to calm the situation, 'I do not see the purpose of Sir Richard sending his man to talk to me.'

'He is maybe concerned Richenda would respond less civilly to him,' said Muller.

'Plant him a facer,' said Richenda crudely.

'I think we have lingered long enough over the table,' said Mrs Muller. 'We should all retire to the drawing-room for tea.'

Muller gave a mock groan. 'We do not have to drink tea after every meal, Mother.'

'It is the English thing to do,' said his mother stubbornly in her perfect English. I looked at her sharply. Why had she been so obviously, even comically, German in front of my mother?

As if reading my thoughts. Richenda commented excitedly. 'We had the most intriguing visitor this afternoon. The daughter of an earl, no less.'

'Then we must invite her to the ball,' said Muller, rising and pulling out Richenda's chair for her.

'I doubt she would come,' I said quickly. 'She is widowed with a young son.'

'You know her?' asked Muller.

'I have heard of her,' I answered quickly. 'Staff talk.'

'Not mine,' said Mrs Muller, blissfully unaware that the task of keeping her four hundred staff from gossiping is not humanly possible, but I assured her it was a morsel from my Stapleford Hall days.

'Not out of the top drawer,' muttered Mrs

Muller as she left the room. Her son followed her quickly and we heard urgent whispering. Richenda blushed and, showing unusual tact, held back for a moment.

'Whatever have I done wrong, Euphemia?' she asked. 'Only this morning Mrs Muller praised my fashion sense and she wasn't being ironic!'

'Could she have been jealous of your conversation with your visitor?' I could not bring myself to give my mother's name.

'I would have introduced her,' said Richenda close to tears. 'I honestly thought she was asleep and when I first met the woman I had no idea she was aristocracy. She looked so – so drab.'

Considering Richenda's fashion sense my mother would have taken this as a compliment. However my current mistress looked close to hysteria. I cast about in my mind frantically to think of something to distract her. An hysterical Richenda is not something even the strongest man should bear witness to. 'Barker, your brother's man, said Muller killed his first wife.' As soon as it was out of my mouth I knew I had said the wrong thing.

Richenda's eyes went very wide. 'Oh no, Euphemia,' she said in awed tones, 'you haven't discovered another body, have you? That would be too much. Everyone should have a hobby, but...'

'No, of course not,' I snapped. 'Richard is afraid you will marry Muller and he will get his hands on your bank shares.' I coughed and added, 'I mean that literally and not as a euphemism.'

'A what?' said Richenda blankly, 'Come on, we should join Muller. Whether his mother likes me or not, I'm damn well going to this ball. I have this idea for a deep purple silk dress with lemon puffed sleeves...'

I followed Richenda through the drawing room, trying desperately hard not to imagine what she was describing, but her notion of sartorial elegance once envisaged tended to engrave itself on one's mind to the extent that I often woke in the night in a cold sweat fearing she had taken it upon herself to design a dress for me. This disturbed me more than my dreams of finding a body in the corridor of Stapleford Hall. Really, I was becoming almost accustomed to corpses.

The evening ended in a long discussion about the autumn ball. I was dragooned into doing much of the donkey work. Not the actual physical moving for plants and tables, but the labour intensive copper-plate writing of invitations and discussing beforehand with Mrs Muller who should be invited to the dinner and where they should all sit. Gentlemen tend not to realise how difficult and fraught this task can be, merely trusting to their womenfolk that everyone will be happily arranged. I think it is a great pity that they therefore do not have the sense to let us run the Foreign Office.

Richenda gave loads of impractical suggestions and Muller seemed to be at pains to give in to her wishes. Though even he blanched at her prospective colour scheme for the ballroom – to compliment her as yet unmade dress. I gave him a small nod, signifying I would interfere in this matter and he gave an audible sigh of relief.

'What is the matter, Hans? Are you tired?'

asked his mother.

'Indeed, it has been a long trip from London and I am ready to retire,' replied our quick-thinking host. And with that a line was drawn under the proceedings. It was understood that Mr Muller would be supplying the funds, but from now on the ball was the women's affair. I thought he arranged this very neatly.

As I climbed into bed that night I could not help thinking that if anyone could arrange a murder neatly it would be the charming and impeccable Mr Muller. I silently cursed Barker for putting the thought in my head. Of course I then had to get out of bed and pray for Barker to become a nicer man. Murder and the Staplefords may have changed me, but you cannot stop a vicar's daughter being a vicar's daughter. Especially if she almost believes her dead father is looking over her shoulder watching her actions. Not that I do, of course. My father undoubtedly earned his place in heaven simply for living with my mother as long as he did, but once one has been imbued with a beloved parent's belief system it is difficult to run contrary to it.

I was kneeling on the floor, on a rather comfortable rug, trying to find kind words for the despicable Barker, when someone scratched at my door. Now, with this large a staff, it was not impossible that one of the younger, brasher males might try his luck in the women's quarters. My door was tightly bolted so I ignored it. I continued to search for words other than despicable, rogue, thuggish and nasty to describe Barker. The scratching continued to the point that my concentration snapped. 'Oh, do go away,' I cried. 'I'm trying to be nice about someone horrible!'

'Why would you want to do that,' came Richenda's voice from beyond the door. I sighed and got up and unbolted the door.

'Why didn't you just say it was you?'

'I'm being discreet,' said my mistress. 'And why are you being nice about horrid people and to whom?' She looked around the room puzzled.

'I was praying.'

Richenda looked somewhat startled. 'Isn't that what Sundays are for?'

'What do you want?'

'I've heard something in the attic and I think it must be Muller's wife,' said Richenda.

I fetched over my candle from the table, so I could see her more clearly. Her cheeks did not appear flushed. 'Did you have a lot of wine at dinner?' I asked bluntly.

Richenda gave a little snort. 'Don't be rude,' she said. 'I was reading in bed when I quite clearly heard a crash above me.'

'A servant falling out of bed?'

Richenda shook her head. 'There are no servants' quarters above where I sleep. Muller designed the main bedrooms so no servants could be within earshot at any time of day or night.' She added, 'There are bells, of course.'

'So you're saying there is nothing but storage above your bedroom?'

'No, it wasn't simply something falling over,' said Richenda. 'It was moving.'

'Moving luggage?'

Richenda stamped her foot. 'Damn you, take me

seriously! Don't you think it odd that a man would design a wing out of earshot of his servants?'

'Not if he wanted privacy.'

'Exactly! He's hiding something.'

'But he put you over there!'

'Stop splitting hairs and come with me!' demanded Richenda. 'Remember, I pay your wages!'

I sighed and picked up a shawl to wrap around myself. 'Bring the candlestick,' said Richenda. 'It will make a good weapon.'

'Not as good as you would think,' I muttered trailing after her. I had had experience with the fallibility of candlesticks.

It may be that many servants would have parted company at this point with their mistress, but to me a midnight stroll through a strange attic was a positive breeze compared to when I had first met Richenda and she had asked me to drag her cousin's body, by the leg, out of a corridor and into the light so we 'could have a really good look'.

Without pride, I can say it would have to be an atticful of bodies to discomfort me. Richenda led me to her bedroom and threw open the door. 'Listen!' The room looked as if it had been ransacked and smelt slightly of underwashed garments. No one could have mistaken it for anyone other than Richenda's room.

I dutifully did as I was bid. After giving it about two minutes – she didn't pay me that much – I was about to suggest it had been a dream when I heard distinct movement above our heads.

'There!' shouted Richenda. 'You heard that!'

'Unless you want to wake Mr Muller and ask if he does have a wife stored in the attic, I suggest you keep your voice down,' I said with a calmness I was far from feeling.

Richenda giggled nervously. Her face went blotchy. I made a mental note to warn her not to do that in public. 'So how do we get up there?' I asked.

Richenda frowned. 'I assumed being a servant you would know.'

'I'm not that kind of a servant any more,' I said.

'But don't you still know?' persisted Richenda.

The attic rumbled above us and we both jumped.

'You mean by some divinely inspired lower-class sense?' I snapped.

'How would I know,' cried Richenda. 'I wasn't born in that world!'

I barely bit back the words 'neither was I' before a noise like rolling thunder echoed down the chimney. 'Are you sure you want to go up there?' I said.

'Of course,' said Richenda. 'but you're going first. You've got the candle.'

'Our deadly weapon,' I said. This time Richenda laughed. Then she sighed. 'I don't really think it's Muller's last wife, you know. Or at least I wouldn't think that if it wasn't half past three in the morning and we weren't standing here in our petticoats in the near dark. It's just that sometimes the setting...'

'Unleashes your imagination?' I said.

'And this wing of the house is odd.'

'Modern design?' I suggested.

'Or he ran out of money,' said Richenda. 'That's the kind of thing I need to know if I'm to

42

accept his proposal.'

'He's proposed?'

'I shouldn't think he's even thought of it yet,' said Richenda, 'but he's coming round. The autumn ball.'

'It's like he is putting on a show for you,' I agreed.

There was a soft, but distinct noise above us. 'So you see,' said Richenda. 'I do need to know if he has any secrets in his attic.'

The hairs stood up on the back of my neck as the faint sound continued above us. I attempted to catch Richenda's lighter tone though I had begun to shiver. 'And if he murdered his wife?' I asked.

'Even you, with your ability to attract murder, must admit that to come from one household where there was one confirmed murder and one murder disguised as a suicide, must agree that the chances of us stumbling on another murder within a month are slight.'

'I suppose it depends on the circles you move in,' I said gloomily.

'But my brother isn't involved in this!' said Richenda, which was as close as she would probably ever come to admitting what her brother was capable of doing.

'He and Muller have been friends for years,' I said.

'Richard does not go around murdering everyone he meets,' said Richenda. 'We'd have no friends or family left.'

I thought it prudent at this point to suggest that we hunted for the stairway. I persuaded Richenda to take her own candle by promising I would still go first if we found the attic and we set off to tiptoe through the hallways.

Now, when a house-party is in progress it is very easy to tiptoe around the bedrooms. I fear I must explain why. It is not uncommon for those of the upper classes to seek to change bedroom accommodation during the night for extra – er – entertainment. It is therefore an unwritten rule that noises in corridors are ignored. However, this was not a house party. Richenda was the only guest in residence. (I didn't count.) And I believe both Muller and his mother would be shocked if she sneaked about in the night. I had no way of knowing if Muller would welcome such an advance or, as many men would be, be frightened by it. Richenda had her hair in rags and was at her most gorgonlike. Either way to be caught was unacceptable for either of us.

So like a pair of inept, but very, very cautious burglars, we checked up and down the hallway. Muller's bedroom lay at the end of the hallway and I assumed must be a set of rooms, considering how the outside of the building was formed – or as much as I could recall of it in the middle of the night. His mother's room was two doors away. We could hear her snoring and Richenda's room had been two doors further away than that. In all there were eight bedrooms on the corridor.

The carpet lay charitably thick and plush beneath our slippered feet, but as we walked down the corridor we could see no exit but the stairs down.

'Perhaps there is a secret passageway,' whispered Richenda.

'Perhaps one of the bedrooms isn't a bedroom,' I said.

'How do we tell which one?' asked Richenda.

'Well, if I was going to hide a secret staircase to a secret attic, I would do it close to my own room if not in it.'

'We cannot enter Muller's bedroom,' squeaked Richenda.

'No,' I agreed. 'Let's check the doors either side. If it's neither of them I think we should count ourselves lucky we haven't been caught and go back to bed. I'll swap rooms with you tonight if you want. There are definitely no noises above mine.'

'That will not be necessary,' said Richenda haughtily.

Richenda took the door to the left of Muller's room and I the one to the right. Even by the candlelight I could see her steeling herself. Then very slowly, with her fingers widely splayed, she opened the door. Her other hand trembled as she held up the candle to peer inside. Then she closed the door and turned to me. 'Bedroom,' she mouthed.

I turned the handle of my door and leant gently on the door at the same time to help prevent the hinges from groaning. But like everything in this house the hinges were well-looked-after and well-oiled. The door gave easily. A cold gust of air blew out my candle flame. Richenda crept to my side and held her candle aloft.

Stairs.

Chapter Six

The Creature in the Attic

With her usual flair Richenda moved her candle into exactly the place where I had held mine aloft and it too guttered and went out. Richenda uttered a small squeak which would have been much louder if I hadn't stuck my hand over her mouth. I reckoned a companion got to take far more liberties than a maid, especially when we were outside the bedroom door of a potential wife-murderer.

Richenda's pale blue eyes widened and rolled and for one dreadful moment I thought she was going to faint. I feared considerable injury if she landed on me. But I did the lady an injustice. She pulled my hand none too gently away from her face, scowled ferociously, and whispered, 'What do we do now?'

Neither of us having interest in tobacco, we did not carry any means of making fire on our persons. 'Do you want to go back?' I asked. Richenda shook her head. 'The moon's bright tonight.'

'That won't help us in an attic,' I answered.

'In this one it will,' said Richenda deepening her voice, presumably in an effort to sound ominous, 'there are windows. I checked from the outside. If you walk over in the woods on the left just before the tree-line you can see up far enough to see them.'

'That's odd,' I said.

Richenda nodded.

'Is there any reason we're doing this in the middle of the night?' I asked. 'We could wait until Muller goes back to town and his mother is having her afternoon nap.'

'I didn't think you would be chicken,' said Richenda.

I sighed. 'You have to admit I am awfully good at coming across the unpleasant and unexpected.' I said. 'I'm sure daylight would make it easier.'

'Personally, if Muller has shut his mad wife up in the attic, I'd rather discover her when she was asleep,' said Richenda.

I agreed she had a point. Cautiously I mounted the first stair. Of course, it creaked. Wait until Richenda stands on you, I thought down at it, you'll positively groan. I moved on quickly, not convinced the treads would take the weight of both of us at once. The staircase was no darker than the rest of the house and my eyes were beginning to adjust when we were plunged into pitch-darkness.

'I closed the door,' hissed Richenda in my ear. 'We don't want anyone following us up.'

'I can't see a thing,' I protested.

'Oh, let me,' said Richenda.

There followed some complicated tussling as we manoeuvred for position. If Richenda wanted to go first I had no objection. I had begun to get a very bad feeling about this plan. We squeezed past each other in the dark. Richenda, though large, proved to be squishy without her numerous usual

47

strappings. I got a bit breathless at one point and seriously considered it might be better to pitch down the stairs than to have my lungs flattened out against the wall, but the moment passed and she was ahead of me.

'Right,' breathed Richenda, and she gave a little snort not unreminiscent of a horse anticipating a good gallop. 'We're off!'

As if to prove her superior fearlessness and excellent night vision she set off at a fast pace. I lagged cautiously behind her. Now we had tested the width of the passageway against our frames I wanted warning if I needed to press myself against the wall as she tumbled past.

In my defence I will say that Richenda had considerably more padding than my bonier self and was less likely to come to serious injury. Besides, now I was in the rear I found myself unreasonably peeved. Usually when I made night-time discoveries I was in the lead. Mentally I scolded myself for being prideful, but as a servant one has very few distinguishing characteristics. I rather liked being the brave and bold one. Obviously not too bold. I am a vicar's daughter after all. My internal musings were cut short by Richenda sneezing. If you have ever heard a horse sneeze you know the sound. While not overly loud it is pronounced and liable to be moist. I hung back.

The air tasted dry and stale in my mouth. Dust tickled my nose. Reason asserted itself. No one came up here. Even a mad wife would need to be fed over a period of three years. I opened my mouth to share this insight with Richenda, but I was cut off by a loud thump. Sense fled. My heart beat frantically, but I pressed my lips tight so no sound could escape.

A most unladylike exclamation came from above. 'There's a hatch,' said Richenda. 'I just found it with my head.'

'Is it bolted?' I asked.

'Wait a mo,' said Richenda. 'I'm feeling around the edges. Hmm. There it is.'

I heard a rusty bolt being pulled back and then came a bang that must surely wake anyone below as Richenda threw open the hatch. 'Quick!' she cried and scrambled up. 'Before anyone comes.' I had a sudden mental image of us both standing over the closed hatch, candlesticks aloft to preserve our virtue. Giggles bubbled inside me.

With the hatch open the darkness thinned. It thickened momentarily as Richenda's posterior filled the hatchway and then lightened. I hurried up after her. Richenda shut the hatch after me. 'So we have warning if anyone comes,' she said. I set down my useless candlestick.

Moonlight flooded the attic casting a landscape of shapes and shadows around us. I looked out one of the big round windows. The ground below lay wide and silver in the moonlight. Grass. Not even prickly bushes. Not an escape exit then; unless I pushed Richenda first and landed on her.

I heard Richenda behind me moving across the room, muttering to herself. I turned and tried to make sense of the shapes around us. She really did have much better night-sight than me. The attic was huge. We seemed to be at the end of this wing, and, I realised with a shudder, directly above Muller's bedroom. Three round windows allowed the moonlight to flood in from the end wall, but the attic stretched on and on. It appeared to contain the whole of this wing without division. Or so I suspected. Bright though the moonlight was, it could not penetrate the most remote corners. Across the floor were not simply boxes, but I could make out the outline of a desk and some bookcases against the walls. It looked as if the attic was indeed intended for habitation. I feared the worst.

'Richenda,' I hissed at her disappeared shadow. 'Come back. Someone's up here.'

Nothing.

'Richenda!'

I placed my hand against the wall and began to inch along, skirting the objects I could see. Nevertheless my feet frequently came into contact with hard immovable objects. When they did, I put my hands on them and edged my way round. It would be all too easy to lose my balance. To my surprise most of the things I touched felt soft. Dust, I thought, until I felt a prickling sensation across my hand. Spider webs. Spider webs and spiders. If I never saw another attic again it'd be fine by me.

Richenda still continued on, despite my hissed implorings for her to stop. Twice I edged my way around a chimney. At least there were no open fireplaces. I moved as quietly as I could and strained my ears for any sound. I particularly listened for the creaking of the hatch, but Richenda's footfalls echoed loudly in the darkness. If there was anyone or anything here it must surely have heard us. I began to feel about me for a weapon. Then I heard it. The sound of a falling body.

'Ooofff!' said Richenda. 'I think I've found a fireplace.'

I made my way across as quickly as I could. Richenda lay in a pool of darkness, a combination of soot and shadow. The fireplace was modest, but I didn't miss that a poker set stood to one side. 'Are you hurt?' I asked.

'No. This was a ridiculous idea, wasn't it?'

'Um – yes.'

'Then why in the world did you let me go ahead?'

I said nothing, but helped pick some of the larger pieces of soot out of her hair. I was about to suggest we took advantage of our luck so far and made our escape, when the rumbling sound we had heard in Richenda's room filled the attic. In the stillness of the night it sounded loud as thunder.

'What the hell!' said Richenda.

'The chimney. It's coming from the chimney.'

'It can't be,' said Richenda and, before I could stop her, she grabbed the poker and stuck it and her head up the chimney. 'Hi you!' she cried. 'Come down here this instant!'

There was a rumbling, a clattering and the rushing sound of falling soot. Richenda staggered out and backwards as a creature burst out from the chimney. It squawked and shot across the room in a cloud of soot and feathers.

'Pigeon,' said Richenda, sitting down in a barely controlled fall.

The bird, completely panicked, flapped and swooped and dived around us. I hauled Richenda to her feet (no mean feat) and pulled her back with me to the end of the attic where we had begun our adventure. I felt her shaking. 'It's all right,' I said. 'It can't harm us.'

'Pigeon,' said Richenda again and I realised she was shaking with laughter. I opened one of the round windows and the pigeon left the building. We both sat down and gave way to mirth.

We were laughing so loudly we didn't hear anyone approaching until the hatch was thrown back. Muller appeared, a broken gun on one arm and a lantern in his other hand. He set the lantern down and snapped the gun shut. The look on his face was dark and thunderous.

He pointed the gun straight at Richenda and me.

Chapter Seven

Revelations

'H-h-Hans?' stuttered Richenda.

Muller broke the gun at once and set it down. Now I was no longer mesmerised by the weapon I was sure a moment ago was about to send me to my doom, I took in Muller's full and rather glorious appearance. He wore a green garment, something between a smoking jacket and a dressing gown. Embroidered golden dragons swooped and dived across it. It shimmered by the light of his lantern. On this feet were matching slippers and his legs were clad in green pyjamas of a similar hue. His short brown hair, greying at the sides, without its usual hair oil, curled around his face. In this dishevelled state he looked quite the best I had ever seen him. It occurred to me that in everyday life he did his best to appear as normal and as nondescript as possible. This immediately made me think of Fitzroy and spies. (Fitzroy had also once levelled a shotgun in my direction, but in fairness this had been to kill someone behind me. Though I had not known that at the time. See my journal *A Death in the Highlands* for the full story.)

'Richenda,' he said in astonished accents. 'Euphemia too? What in God's name are you doing up here?'

'We heard an intruder,' said Richenda in a throbbing accent.

'It was a pigeon,' I explained. Richenda shot me a deathly look for ruining the mood.

'Why the devil didn't you wake me?' demanded Muller.

'I didn't feel it would be appropriate for me to come to your room.' said Richenda in a strangely breathy voice. I assumed she was trying to sound alluring, but honestly it sounded more like she had a bad chest cold. 'Besides, Euphemia has much experience of going about in the dark.'

Muller raised an eyebrow at me and I had to suppress a chuckle. 'You could have summoned a servant to fetch me,' he said not unreasonably.

'I didn't want to disturb you,' said Richenda, still trying to be weak and feminine. As this was rather like a shire horse trying to skip like a lamb she wasn't awfully successful. But it was a better response than admitting we were checking to see if he had locked his last wife up in the attic.

'Could we possibly continue this discussion downstairs?' I asked.

'Of course,' said Muller at once. 'I don't know what I was thinking. Please, ladies, descend.' And he gestured to the stairs.

Once we were all back on the landing, Muller turned on the gas light. 'It is not my usual practice to chat to ladies in the middle of the night, but I think we should take a cup of tea together in the morning room. Please meet me there. I need to lock away the gun.'

Richenda and I exchanged looks. Then Richenda nodded. We both smelled a mystery. Muller waited until we left then we heard him open his door. 'Am I sooty?' hissed Richenda.

'No, not really. Am I?'

'Why would that matter?' said Richenda rudely.

'So you are eager to win his affections,' I said.

Richenda bit her lip. 'If we can rule out the wife-murderer thing.'

I nodded, unaccountable mirth bubbling inside me. 'That does seem sensible.'

We had reached the ground floor by now. Both of us too caught up in our discussion to be even remotely disturbed by shadows.

'Oh damn it, Euphemia,' said Richenda, 'I'm not getting any younger. My brother is – well whatever he is, he is not a saint.'

'No,' I agreed wholeheartedly. 'I…'

'Listen. I'm not like you. I come from a different class. Women my age need to be established. I've only a couple more years and people will be talking about me as a confirmed spinster. I want a family, dammit. I want a place in society. I cared for Tippy, but he's gone and there's nothing I can do about that. Muller's alive and he's clearly looking for a wife.'

'Have you fallen in love with him?' I asked quietly as I opened the door to the morning room. I turned on the gas lamps.

Richenda snorted. 'No, I have not. I barely know the man. I do find him charming.' she admitted.

'Everyone does,' I said.

Richenda brushed my comment away like I was a fly. 'He behaves like a gentleman and I have no doubt he would treat his wife with consideration and the proper respect. But his mother, even when she isn't pretending to have that dreadful accent...'

'Why does she do that?' I interrupted.

'No idea. Batty as a fruitcake if you ask me. But the point is, I can make Muller richer. I can offer him the shares in the bank. I can give him children. And I know how to behave.'

I looked at her blankly.

'Do I need to spell it out? If he marries me I know how to look the other way should he ever require extra – er – activities.'

It took me a moment to catch on. 'Mistresses, you mean?' I gasped.

'I'm not a beauty,' said Richenda staunchly, 'but I could make him a good wife and I think we would make good companions. With all the chaos that has happened to my family and been caused by my family I think he's my last shot.'

She lifted her chin in defiance, but I thought I saw she was blinking back tears. I looked away. 'Where is that maid with the tea?' I said.

Richenda blinked hard. 'Indeed.'

'Richenda, would you object if I repinned some of your hair? It has come down a little. A lady should always look her best.'

'Thank you, Euphemia.' It was the first time I felt Richenda was being sincere. Who would have thought that an incident with a pigeon in an attic could lead to me feeling sorry for a woman I had, if not hated, largely despised.

I had just finished redoing her hair and discreetly wiping away a smut or two when the door opened again to reveal the extraordinary sight of Muller carrying a tea tray. I hurried to take it from him. I have no very great opinion of gentlemen carrying china. By and large they are far too clumsy, not being trained, because of their station, to do the simple things in life. Their hands also tend to be overly large for delicate work.

'Thank you, Euphemia,' said Muller. 'Would you mind pouring for us? I know enough of your history to believe, of the two of you, that you are the least disturbed by this incident.'

I smiled. 'Shall I take that as compliment?'

Muller had the sense not to answer, but only smile. I could feel Richenda beginning to bristle at my side. I poured tea for us all and added milk and sugar as necessary. I noted that Muller didn't know Richenda that well as he had not thought to bring cake or biscuits. Richenda always improves with cake. I was taking my first cup of tea when Muller said, 'I must confess when I realised it was you two ladies in the attic my first thought was that you were looking for my first wife.'

Richenda snorted tea down her nose. Muller

pretended not to notice. 'I thought it likely that, in an attempt to get you to return to Stapleford Hall, Barker would spread malicious gossip about me.'

I felt myself blushing.

'I also thought that as Euphemia is very loyal to you, despite what she may personally think she would feel duty bound to pass on your brother's message.'

You see, he really was a charming man. He had skilfully exonerated me from being a gossip.

'Why would we think your wife was in the attic?' asked Richenda, who was far less capable of playing the diplomat.

Muller sat back in his seat. He looked into the empty fireplace for a moment before refocusing on us. 'There were many rumours around the time of my wife's death. The fact that my father was German and that there is growing ill-will between our two countries has not helped.'

'There is?' asked Richenda. I said nothing. Fitzroy had told me a number of disturbing rumours in order to enforce my complicity in his schemes. I was only surprised that Muller was so aware. As far as I knew he spent all his time in England.

'I am also new money,' said Muller. 'I am a bank director rather than an owner of a bank and while I have invested wisely I am not one of the old school.'

'But you went to the same school as my brother,' said Richenda.

'He means he is not descended from one of the known English families,' I explained.

'Neither am I,' said Richenda. 'Well. Mama was a Lady, but her links are mainly with France.'

Muller nodded. 'Socially you are far above me, Richenda.'

'I daresay my brother will continue in his ways and bring our family name down,' said Richenda bitterly.

Muller was silent.

'What were these rumours?' I asked.

'Everything from my poisoning my wife to locking her in the attic and faking her funeral.'

'But to what end?' I asked.

'I have no idea what is in the heads of my detractors,' said Muller flatly. 'I loved my wife very much. It was not in my mother's eyes a great match as she came from a respectable, but middle-class, family, and Mother had high hopes for me to do better. But truthfully I always felt it was not a good match for my wife as, for all my upbringing, I am accounted a foreigner. We met when I was building the estate and I had never seen a more pretty and fragile creature. I was some years her senior, but for no obvious reason she fell in love with me and I asked her to marry me. For the few years we were together we were. I believe, both very happy. The only sadness was that we had no children. My wife was pregnant several times...' he swallowed hard, 'but God granted us no live children.'

'I'm sorry,' I said.

'I fear she was too frail. That those failed pregnancies took too great a toll. I have often felt as if I did indeed murder her. I should have ... but she, too, so wanted children.'

'I thought it was a heart attack that took her from you,' I asked as gently as I could.

'That is what our family doctor put on her death certificate, but I have blamed myself these three years for her death.'

Richenda reached awkwardly across the table and touched Muller lightly on the hand. 'For the little it is worth I think you have nothing to reproach yourself for. I think that your wife was lucky you loved her so much. Few women have the luxury of such a marriage as you describe.'

Muller looked up and into her eyes. 'Thank you,' he said. 'You are very kind.'

'And my brother is a pig,' said Richenda totally breaking the tragic-romantic mood with hard reality. 'I knew he was a rotter in the nursery, but being twins we always supported each other. But no more. I am only sorry he has been the cause of this distress. I quite understand if you would like us to leave. Euphemia and I.'

'No,' said Muller, shaking his head. 'I won't hear of it. I will not be the one responsible for sending you back to that man. I know it would be difficult for you to stay here indefinitely...'

'You mean people will begin to talk,' said Richenda blushing a fiery red. Fortunately the gas light toned the awfulness of her blush down. Red hair and red skin is not a good look.

'But until you have some plan for your future I offer whatever protection you require.'

'Thank you,' said Richenda.

Goodness. That was the second time she had been sincere in the same evening. Could it be that Richenda was genuinely beginning to break away from her brother's influence?

Chapter Eight

Misgivings

Richenda and I both came down for breakfast somewhat later than usual. The maid told us Mrs Muller had already completed her meal and had gone out to walk the gardens with Mr Bennie. Mr Muller had also breakfasted. He sent his compliments and regrets that he would not be available again until dinner time as he had to spend the day with his factor attending to estate business. I guessed he intended to give us time to think over our position or he might also be assessing his own intentions towards Richenda. I had liked her better than ever before last night, but she had looked a fright. He could well be testing his resolve to face her gorgon-style night hair in intimate situations. I have no experience of bedroom intimacies. Hope as well as sense tells me a man can love or desire a woman for who she is inside her fleshy shell, but a man, reasonably enough, does not expect to be frightened in his bedchamber.

When the maid withdrew I buttered myself a slice of toast and said airily, 'So just us, Richenda. Shall we explore the rest of the attics?'

Richenda gave a shudder. 'I don't believe I ever want to enter another attic again in my life,' she said. 'But there are some things I think we should look into.'

'Oh,' I said, misgivings flooding through me.

'I think the death of Muller's wife bears a little more research.'

'Oh for goodness' sake, Richenda, haven't we troubled the poor man enough? He opened his heart to you last night and broached what must have been a very painful subject. This is how you repay his confidence?' This was a very forthright speech for a companion. I can only offer as my defence that my brain was too tired to censor my words. That and the fact I had found Muller very affecting.

'Are you attracted to Muller too?' spat Richenda.

'No,' I answered slightly too quickly. The truth was I found Muller surprisingly restful to be around. In recent years I had been surrounded by men who suffered from being murderous, passionate or jealous. Charm proved to be a pleasant change and even I had to admit that when he wasn't trying to look perfect the English gentleman he was rather attractive. 'All right, I confess I find him charming,' I said, 'but leaving that aside he'd never look as low for a bride as me...'

'I don't know why,' snapped Richenda, 'Wasn't his wife the sister of a vicar or something?'

'I only want to marry for love.'

'Oh,' said Richenda. 'I didn't realise you were a romantic.'

'An incurable one, I'm afraid.'

'So we are not in competition?'

In a thousand years I would never have dreamed that Richenda would ask me such a question. 'We are not,' I said with perfect truth.

'Good,' said Richenda. 'Because you are much

prettier than me.' I gasped at this admission.

'I'm not blind,' said Richenda snappily. 'Of course you have neither my fashion sense nor my money, so I have the advantage.'

'Of course,' I managed to say in a small voice, keeping a straight face.

'I need you to help me find out what is going on here.'

'I don't think there is anything going on,' I said. 'Honestly. I'm enjoying the peace and quiet.'

'H-rumff,' snorted Richenda. 'Why then was I one minute flavour of the month and the next Mrs Muller has no time for me and you're the one helping organise the ball.'

'Please,' I said, 'take that duty from me. It will be dull and tedious and long. Mostly writing invitations in copperplate.'

'Oh, I don't want to do it,' said Richenda. 'I wanted her to want me to do it.'

'Oh.'

'And that ridiculous display of German-ness the other afternoon. Just as I was getting acquainted with the Duke's daughter.'

'Earl's,' I corrected automatically. Richenda gave me a startled look. 'Much lower rank,' I added, 'if that's any consolation.'

'I suppose so. I never did pay that much attention to that kind of stuff at finishing school.' I suspected it was more that the daughters of noble houses paid no attention to her, a banker's daughter, only recently ennobled. No one hated the nouveau riche more than the impoverished nobility.

'Does it matter?' I asked. 'I believe she is not a

permanent resident in the neighbourhood.' Richenda shrugged. 'It was bizarre and ... and mean.'

'Maybe she is simply old,' I suggested gently.

'Batty, you mean? Well, I want to know that too if I end up marrying into this family.'

I gave her a very level look and she returned it. 'You're serious, aren't you?'

'As I said last night this may well be my last chance. If you help me, Euphemia, I won't forget it.'

I didn't answer simply because I couldn't think of what to say. Richenda lent forward. 'I'm sorry we haven't always seen eye to eye. I have always followed my brother's lead and that hasn't been wise. And I haven't been happy for a long time. You haven't known me at my best.'

'Yes,' I said. Then coughed. 'I mean no.'

'Let's start again,' said Richenda. 'I'm sure I will do something awful sooner or later, but this time if I do, it won't be deliberate.' She gave me a shrewd look. 'I am aware that both of us are somewhat adrift in a man's world. Different rivers perhaps, but we both have to look to our own survival.'

'Yes, that's true,' I admitted. 'Did you really set up a house for fallen women?'

'And did I do it simply to annoy my father?' Richenda studied her bacon closely then shoved the better part of a rasher in her mouth and chewed. I waited for her to speak. Goodness, but the woman made a lot of noise when she ate! 'Yes, I wanted to annoy my father. When he married Bertram's mother I was very young, but even then

I felt he was disrespecting my mother's memory. My late stepmother was a hideous snob, who got fed up of living in genteel poverty. She didn't care for my father and I don't believe he cared for anything but her money. I have no idea how he felt about my mother, but I have a few memories of her being kind to me. Of a gentle woman, who never raised her voice. So of course I decided that she had to have been the better woman. My stepmother made no pretence that I was anything but an inconvenience and made it clear that my looks were – inferior. How Bertram turned out so well I have no idea.' Richenda blinked hard. 'I am getting away from your question. Yes, I disliked my father and I wanted to irk him. I did also feel, and still do, that women have a hard time in this world and that this is generally the fault of men. I had a little legacy from my godmother. Not much, but I endowed a house to help fallen women and by that I mean everyone from prostitutes to pregnant maids. One of my main aims was to find a way whereby women would not be separated from their illegitimate children. I'm sorry if that shocks you, but I have always felt that every child deserves a loving mother.'

'Because you lost yours?' I asked.

Richenda nodded. 'Now this is getting downright maudlin.' She took a deep breath. 'And I was jealous of you. You turned the heads of every man when you entered our house and I thought you were taking advantage of that.'

I spluttered tea indignantly. 'I know,' continued Richenda, 'I was wrong. You are as much a victim as me, except you are so very pretty.'

'Thank you,' I said. 'Not for the compliment, but for being so honest with me.'

'It doesn't come naturally,' said Richenda ruefully. 'But Muller gave me a good example to follow last night.'

I nodded. 'He is a very good man.'

'Or does a good job of pretending to be one,' said Richenda. 'Being hoodwinked by my brother for years has made me a little distrustful, but you hit the nail on the head when you said how very charming he is. Everyone says it. Richard once told me he is known as the most charming man in the city. He's never been known to raise his voice or be anything other than even-tempered. Now that isn't natural. Even if he is a foreigner.'

'You don't trust him, but you want to marry him?'

'I believe that is the normal marital state,' answered Richenda. 'But I would like to be totally clear he didn't have anything to do with murdering his wife.'

'Other than by getting her pregnant too often.'

'Euphemia, such things are not spoken of!'

Several retorts sprung to my tongue ranging from commenting how much like my mother she sounded to that such things should jolly well be talked about, but admittedly not by us. Instead, I kept my thoughts to myself for once and only said, 'What do you want me to do?'

'Not much,' admitted Richenda. 'It happened a while ago and she's buried. We can hardly dig her up.'

'No!' I exclaimed in alarm.

'I said we couldn't,' said Richenda reproachfully. 'I was thinking you could ask around the servants. See if there is any gossip. There must have been something off about it for Richard to get Barker to mention it.'

'You don't think your brother was simply trying to cause trouble?'

'Oh, I'm certain of it,' responded his loyal sister. 'But where there's smoke.'

I sighed. 'If it will make you happier I will ask as much as I can without arousing suspicion.'

'Thank you,' said Richenda. 'And when I marry Muller I will keep you on as my companion. After all, he is in the city a great deal and this is the country.' She said the last word with a huge sigh.

I, on the other hand, caught a glimmer of what could be a safe and quiet harbour for the years to come and an assured income for my family.

I should have known my course would never run that smoothly.

Chapter Nine

Secrets and Unexpected Guests

The next day Mrs Muller drew me to one side in the morning room and with much apologising asked me to start on the invitations. 'I should ask Hans to get me a secretary, but most days there would be nothing for her to do.'

'I take it you did not expect your son to restart your ball this autumn?' I asked politely as she handed me a very long list of names and a heavy address book.

'No, it quite took me by surprise. Since the death of my daughter-in-law Hans has not kept an active social life. In the last year he has started spending time with his old school friends and work colleagues, but he hasn't...' She paused delicately.

'Shown any sign that he might be thinking of remarrying?' I finished boldly.

Mrs Muller clutched my hands with her own. I barely held on to my bundle. 'You understand, I am so glad. He loved her, but life must go on and he needs an heir for this fine estate.'

'Of course. It is only natural.'

Mrs Muller continued to grasp at me. 'I am so, so glad you understand. I would not want you to think Hans was fickle.'

'My dear Mrs Muller, I have never thought that,' I said, wondering why on earth it should matter to her if I did. I am, after all, hired help.

'Excellent. Please use the morning room for your work. As you see the fire has been lit. I must now go and arrange with the cook what we need to serve and of course what we need to order.'

'Will you be having flowers?' I asked. 'Autumn is not the best time for floral decorations.'

'Oh, Bennie will sort something out. He has been with us for ages and is a most excellent gardener.'

I lowered my voice. 'It was he who found her, was it not?' I was definitely treading on dangerous ground here, so I added quickly, 'He must be exceptionally loyal to stand by you through such a difficult time.' Etiquette-wise I could be burning my bridges with Mrs Muller. I studied her re-action closely.

A number of different emotions crossed her face, but she settled into a gentle smile. This time she laid a hand on my arm. 'No one should underestimate the value of loyal staff. Why some of them become like family.'

'How lovely,' I said, moving backward out of reach. 'I must start on these cards.'

'Excellent, dear,' said Mrs Muller and left.

I sighed and settled down at the small writing desk. It took some effort to arrange the list, book, and cards in a manner that I could consult them, write neatly, and not knock everything on the floor. I had no doubt that somewhere Hans Muller had an excellent desk, just as I had little doubt I would not be allowed to use it. I had to make do with this inadequate piece of furniture, designed for the lady of the house to dash off little notes. To a man's eyes, preparing for a ball was no trouble at all.

'She likes you,' said a voice from the doorway. I turned round to see Lucy bearing a tray with tea and bread and butter. 'I've been told to bring this up to you to keep up your strength.' She set the tray down on a table in the middle of the room. 'What you doing?'

'Writing invitations for the ball,' I answered shortly.

'He's having a ball!' shouted Lucy. 'The autumn ball? Oh my, I never thought he'd have another.'

With a sinking heart I realised the general staff had obviously not yet been informed. 'Lucy, I shouldn't have said anything. Please don't mention it to the other staff.'

Lucy's eyes shone and she tapped the side of her nose. 'Be our secret,' she said. 'Who's being invited?'

I pointed at the long list on the desk. To my surprise Lucy picked it up and scanned it. Her face fell. 'Only the locals,' she said. 'And to think we used to be good for at least an earl. Some of the dresses of those ladies!' She gave an ecstatic sigh. 'I ain't never seen anything so beautiful.'

'Did the late Mrs Muller dress well?' I asked.

'She wasn't one for very fancy clothes. Didn't come from that background. She dressed pretty rather than posh, if you know what I mean. Respectable.'

'She sounds nice,' I said rather lamely.

'She was. Lovely little thing. Broke her heart that she couldn't carry a child to term.'

'I imagine Mr Muller was just as upset.'

'I think he was more concerned about her. He fell to bits when she died.'

'Poor man.'

'And then those hideous rumours that he had something to do with her death. Cruel, they were, cruel.'

'You don't think he did...' I trailed off under Lucy's fierce glare.

'No, I jolly well don't! I'm not saying there wasn't something strange about her death, but Mr Muller loved her. He'd never have hurt her.'

'Something strange?'

'You're a nosy one, aren't you?'

'Lucy,' I took a deep breath. 'I am only asking because I believe my mistress and your master are growing closer.'

Lucy let out a peal of laughter. 'Her! He wouldn't look at her.'

I did my best to adopt my mother's best look of disapproval. (She still claims she once at eighteen made a Duke cry. Though she still refuses to tell me which one it was.) The effect was wasted on Lucy, who continued to rock with laughter. I did my best to chill my voice as I said, 'I am much attached to my mistress. She has been very good to me.'

Lucy wiped her eyes. 'Ah well, there's none so blind as do not see,' she said cryptically. She wiped her eyes. 'I'm sorry, you're obviously attached to her.' She hesitated. 'The master's valet, Simpson, I had a bit of a crush on him and he told me a lot of stories.' I looked at her blankly. 'Stories about the master and his fondness for pretty women.'

'When he was married?' I asked, shocked. I couldn't imagine Muller as an adulterer, but then that could be the key to his success.

'No,' admitted Lucy. 'Later. I mean after his wife died you wouldn't expect him to live like a monk, would you? He's a gentleman.'

I opted for not diving into those particularly muddy moral waters and asked bluntly, 'What did he tell you?'

'Oh, only that he knew the master favoured small, petite, brunettes. He never told me any real details like, but we was all curious to know if the master was going to marry again. After all a single man doesn't normally keep up a big estate and we was all worried for our jobs.'

'So he told you Muller preferred to entertain

himself elsewhere rather than marry again?'

Lucy shook her head. 'No, he told us when the master felt up to being interested in women again, as it were.'

'How long after his wife's death was this?' I asked. I was beginning to feel very uncomfortable with this topic, but Lucy discussed it with the ease with which I imagine she would have discussed flower arrangements.

'About a year and a half. Simpson said he definitely had a type and all respect due your mistress ain't anything like it.'

'You said there was something strange about his wife's death?' With Lucy in full flow I thought she might finally answer the only question I needed to ask.

Lucy gave me a thoughtful grin. 'What's it worth to you?'

'Excuse me?'

'I reckon if your mistress has got her hooks into him – Lord knows how – then this kind of information would be worth something.' She rubbed her fingers together. 'You know, money.'

'I shall ask Simpson,' I said, as calmly as I could given the sudden sordid turn of events.

'You can't,' said Lucy triumphantly, 'he's left. And I reckon I'm the only one he told. You wants to know. You can pay for the privilege. It's nothing personal, but a girl's got to look out for herself.'

'I see.'

'Look, you make up your mind if you want the information and if you does then meet me in the rose garden after tea and before dinner. That's when both Cook and the housekeeper take their

71

naps. Easier time for me to have a little chat.' She stood up and fluffed out her skirts. 'Now, I've got real work to do,' and she flounced out of the room leaving the 'unlike some' unspoken, but heavy in the air.

I picked up my lists, but I found it difficult to focus. At Stapleford Hall we had all chatted about those above stairs, but I had never come across an instance of anyone attempting to sell information about the family, and in particular their love affairs. Though it is true I had had to once oust a press man from the garden. He had offered me money for information, but then the press are generally composed of a very low sort – or so my mother says.

Perhaps none of us wanted to think of Richard Stapleford as a lover; it was simply too ghastly a concept and would undoubtedly give one nightmares. Strangely it seemed the Stapleford's' servants were far more loyal than those of the charming Muller. The world would never make sense to me. I doubted Lucy had any real information for me. She would have been very young at the time, but perhaps not too young to attract the valet's story. Still, could I take that chance? I would have to approach Richenda about the matter and see what she thought. I certainly was not paying for sordid gossip out of my own money!

Richenda stopped to check up on me shortly before luncheon to ask how I progressed. I told her of my conversation with Lucy. 'Sneaky little cow,' were the first words out of her mouth. Although I would not have put it in such terms, I nodded in agreement. 'Just what we need,' she added. 'How much do you think we should pay her?'

'I have no idea,' I responded.

'Don't look so shocked, Euphemia. It's quite normal for servants to make money out of gossip. Admittedly usually it's between themselves or a lady's maid who is after her mistress's cast-offs. It happens in all the great houses.'

And so it was, much later in the day, that I took a walk in the rose garden between tea and dinner. In the country it is normal practice to eat earlier than in town, but there is still a significant gap of time between the two meals. I wandered about with Richenda's generous donation stowed in my purse and pretended to admire the flowers. After the long hot summer, autumn had come in rather brisk. After an hour I found myself begin to shiver. I had assumed Lucy would have some duties for the dinner period and was most likely to turn up closer to tea time. I was being proved wrong. Bennie, the head gardener, a short, blond-haired man in his mid-fifties had now passed me twice. Each time he had doffed his hat to me, but I felt a third time would arouse his suspicions. He was a dapper little man. Not at all like I had imagined a head gardener to be, but he had reverently introduced himself to me the first time in passing in order to point out the location of the prettiest blooms at this time of year. He became quite animated when he discussed the garden and I was not impervious to the fact that he had a particular kind of charisma when he talked about his work. The gardens were lovely and I had no doubt he inspired the men under his direction. I knew he worked closely with Mrs Muller and I felt certain that should we pass by each other a third time he would be liable to mention to her that I had been walking in the cold gardens alone for a considerable time. He might assume I delighted in his work, but I thought Mrs Muller would be liable to be more suspicious as I had previously shown no interest in the flower gardens or the magnificent floral arrangements in the house. The truth was that being raised as a country girl I loved the bright wildness of the hedgerows and found more formal arrangements stuffy and confining. I was careful not to say this to Bennie.

So I returned to the house cold, irritable and with my mission unaccomplished. I was thinking only of gaining my room and hoping that someone had already lit my fire as I strode across the hall. And so it was I walked into the back of a man standing stock still in the middle of the hall where I simply had not expected to find him, nor had he any business to be...' He turned and caught me by the elbows as we both stumbled about a bit.

'Euphemia!' cried Bertram, for it was he. 'What the hell sort of place is this?'

'Bertram, what are you doing here?' I asked astonished.

'Never mind what I'm doing here!' he said loudly. 'There's a dead parlour maid in the drive.'

Chapter Ten

Unsuitable Scenes

'Oh no! Have you run over Lucy? How many times have I told you, you don't pay enough attention when you are driving?'

'I haven't run over anyone!' snapped Bertram.

I pressed a hand to my face. 'Never tell me it was Merrit!'

'Merrit isn't with me,' said Bertram. 'And nobody has run anyone over.'

'But you said there was a dead parlour maid in the drive.'

'There is!' cried Bertram, clutching his hair in frustration. 'Why is she there?'

'I don't know,' I cried, my voice rising with his. 'If she's dead I shouldn't think she has much say in the matter!'

'Come with me!' demanded Bertram. He snatched me by the wrist and pulled me back out the front door.

'Shouldn't we call the police?' I said, pulling against him, but Bertram would not be stopped. He dragged me round the side where the drive began to unwind towards the house and there, as if some giant hand had pushed her off a bench, lay Lucy, sprawled on the grass. Her limbs were both curled and at the same time at an odd angle, rather like a spider that has gone too near a fire. Her

75

pretty face had contorted into a grimace and well – I am afraid at that point I looked away. Bertram still held my wrist, so I couldn't flee. 'We need to go back to the house,' I said urgently. However, Bertram didn't move. 'My God, she is real. I thought I must've imagined the entire thing. How is it everywhere you go, Euphemia, people die?'

'You found her,' I said hotly. 'The last time I saw her she was very much alive and blackmailing me!'

'Blackmailing you!' said Bertram. 'About what?'

'I was going to pay her for information about the death of Muller's late wife.'

'That's not blackmail,' said Bertram and I heard a certain relief in his voice.

'Did you think I'd killed her?' I asked indignantly.

'Well, you thought I'd killed her,' he responded.

'By accident!' I exclaimed.

We regarded each other angrily. Both of us were breathing fast and our faces were red – at least it felt like I was blushing. 'What are you doing here, anyway?' I demanded. 'Did Richard send you?'

'No,' spat Bertram, 'Muller asked me to come to help protect Richenda's reputation. You think, after everything, I'd do Richard a favour? After he turned you out?'

'And Richenda took me in.'

'Dammit, Euphemia, you know I couldn't. You refused to marry me,' he stumbled over his words. 'If Richenda hadn't taken you I'd have done something. I wouldn't have left you to starve. You know that.'

'Excuse me for interrupting, Miss, Sir,' said the head gardener's voice from behind us, 'but is

Lucy quite well?'

'If you mean the girl lying on the ground,' said Bertram, swinging to face him, 'she's dead.'

'Only I thought I heard an argument,' said Bennie. His blue eyes studied us both closely.

My blush deepened to the heat of a fiery furnace. 'Good heavens,' I said looking at Bertram as I realised how our passions had got the better of us in a very unsuitable way. 'What must you think of us?'

'Oh, he probably thinks we killed her,' said Bertram sitting down on the bench and momentarily dropping his head in his hands. 'Everywhere you go, Euphemia,' he said shaking his head. 'Everywhere you go.'

'If you don't mind,' said Bennie, moving forward, 'I'll check the young lady is properly dead.'

'As opposed to improperly?' asked Bertram sounding near hysterical.

Bennie bent over a Lucy for a moment. Then he straightened and said, 'Yes, I am sorry to say Lucy is dead. I'll get a couple of the garden hands to carry her into the house.'

'You shouldn't move a body,' I blurted out. Bennie looked at me in surprise. 'Not if you think there has been foul play.'

'Who would want to hurt Lucy?' he asked. 'She's a parlour maid. Of no importance to folk like you.'

'I'm sure she was important to someone,' I said in a small, tight voice as I thought how Bertram and I had argued over her body.

Bennie considered me for a moment. 'Then I suppose the proper thing to do is fetch the master of the house. You better do that, Miss. I'll stay here with Lucy and this gentleman.'

'Bertram Stapleford,' said Bertram, 'I arrived a few moments ago. Muller invited me.'

'As you say, sir,' said Bennie. 'The master is in the factor's office. As you go into the stables it is the door on the right, miss. Please don't go disturbing Mrs Muller with this. It'll be shock enough when she hears about it. I don't want her having to deal with the body.'

'Of course,' I said automatically. Bennie gestured towards the stable block, a neat square of buildings that lay at the foot of a shallow hill. They were large enough to appear near, but in reality it took me a good few minutes to reach them, and when I did I was out of breath and my hair had flown loose from its pins.

I ran under the grand archway entrance and opened the first door to my right. I didn't think to knock and so it was I found myself facing a startled Muller and a tall red-haired man in a tweed suit, who were leaning over some plans on a large desk. 'Lucy's dead,' I said breathlessly.

They both spoke at once.

'Who is Lucy?' said Muller.

'Lucy, good God!' said the red-haired man.

And then helpfully I burst into tears. Muller was at my side in an instant, guiding me into a chair and pressing his handkerchief into my hand. 'She's one of the parlour maids, sir,' said the factor.

'How awful,' said Muller. Then he turned his attention again to me and placed one hand lightly on my shoulder. It felt a little beyond appropriate, but at the same time extremely consoling. 'You poor girl,' he said. 'You've had a terrible shock.

Grodin, you must have some brandy in here somewhere. Fetch Miss St John a glass.'

'No, really,' I gulped. People always press brandy on me when I am upset. I hate it.

Muller held the glass to my lips. 'A sip,' he said gently. 'It will help strengthen you.'

I took a sip. As soon as the fiery liquid hit the back of my throat I began to splutter. Muller set the glass down and knelt down beside me. 'Come on, Euphemia,' he said kindly. 'You're made of stronger stuff than this. We need to know how the accident happened. Where...'

I cut him off. 'It wasn't an accident. She's been murdered.'

'Grodin,' said Muller, 'get up to the house and see what's happening. This poor girl is hysterical. Send Lady Richenda to us and I'll meet you up there.'

I heard the bang of the door as Grodin left. Muller got up and sat on the desk in front of me. 'My dear Euphemia, a death is a terrible shock. I know you've had more than your fair share of troubles both at that hunting house in the Highlands and at that terrible wedding fiasco, but you mustn't let your imagination run away with you.' He paused, 'I recognised you from the start, you know.'

His comment struck me like a glass of cold water to the face. 'You knew it was me at The Court?'

Muller nodded. 'Frederick had given me rather a glowing description of you.' He looked faintly embarrassed, but quickly composed himself. 'I thought it was jolly brave of you to back up Richenda like that. I appreciate your loyalty to her. I think you are,' he paused, 'simply outstanding.'

At this point it occurred to me that I was a small brunette of the type Lucy had said Muller preferred. I suddenly felt very vulnerable. Muller smiled again, but made no move towards me.

'Bertram's up at the house,' I blurted out. 'He found Lucy.'

'What an unpleasant introduction to my estate,' said Muller. 'I think I had better take Grodin's brandy with me when we go up.'

'Haven't you...' I begun.

'Yes,' said Muller, plenty of the good stuff in the house, but you know traditionally it's cooking brandy one uses for shock and this isn't far off.' He looked at the label. 'Good Lord, no wonder it made you splutter. I am so sorry, dear girl.'

'Aren't you concerned about Lucy?' I asked, drying my eyes.

'Euphemia, I have over four hundred men and women working on my estate. Nature dictates that occasionally there will be accidents. I am sorry naturally that this has proved to be a lethal one, but death is a sad fact of life. As I know only too well.' He looked down at his hands and sighed.

'Of course, I'm sorry,' I said. 'I didn't mean to remind you.'

Muller shook his head and levelled his gaze to meet mine. 'We both know that after tragedy life continues whether we want it to or not.'

I found myself reaching out a hand to touch his. Entirely inappropriate! But he took my hand in his and gave it a gentle squeeze. 'So no more about murders then?' he said.

What either of us would have said or done next I have no idea. The door flew open and Richenda erupted onto the scene. Instead of dropping my hand, Muller gave it one more squeeze before releasing it in clear sight of Richenda. He then stood.

'What is going on?' said Richenda. She did not sound happy.

'That is exactly what I intend to find out,' said Muller. 'I did not want to leave Euphemia alone. She has had a bad shock. Would you mind escorting her to her bedchamber, Richenda? I don't want the rest of the staff gossiping until we have matters sorted. I believe it was your half-brother who found the body.'

'Bertram!' said Richenda in accents that boded ill for the absent gentleman.

Muller laid a hand on Richenda's shoulder as he passed. 'I knew I could rely on you,' he said and left.

'What an earth is going on?' demanded Richenda of me.

'I'm not sure,' I said slowly, 'but I think the famed Muller charm almost overcame me!'

Chapter Eleven

Death of Innocence

'Almost?' demanded Richenda. 'What were you doing in here before I arrived? You were holding his hand.' If looks could kill.

'I think Lucy's been murdered. Muller didn't

81

want me to keep saying that.'

'So you held hands?' Richenda snorted.

'I thought it was trying to console me,' I said. 'Only now I'm not so sure.'

'You don't think he killed Lucy, do you?'

'He's been with his factor all day. Or at least that is what he told us he was going to do.'

'And who the hell is Lucy anyway?' asked Richenda.

'She's the maid I was going to pay for information.'

'Did you get it?' asked Richenda single-mindedly.

'She didn't meet me…'

'On account of being dead?'

Richenda pulled a captain's chair round from the other side of the desk and sat down with a *whumpf*. The chair creaked alarmingly. 'That's not good,' she said. 'Did you tell Muller about our arrangement?'

I shook my head.

'Good. Don't,' said Richenda. 'People might get the wrong idea.'

'But don't you see she might have been murdered to stop her telling us what she knew?'

'Did you tell anyone about meeting her?'

'Of course not,' I said. 'I'm not a fool. Did you?'

Richenda gave me a look that would have halted an army in its tracks. 'I'm no fool either.'

'No, of course not,' I said quickly. 'But it is odd that she should be killed at the same time as she was meant to be meeting me.'

'You mean highly suspicious,' said Richenda. 'You're sure you didn't tell anyone else about this?'

'No,' I said. 'I wasn't happy about having anything to do with it at all. If you remember.'

'How did she die? How did they do it?'

'I don't know. Bertram came running into the house shouting about a dead maid in the driveway. At first I thought he or Merrit had run her over.'

'Had they?'

'No. Merrit's not here. And she wasn't on the driveway. She was lying on the grass as if she'd tumbled off a stone bench.'

'Pretty cold to be sitting outside,' said Richenda. 'I thought you were meant to be meeting her in the rose garden.'

'I was.'

'Had she hit her head?'

'What? No. She was lying all curled up, but with her limbs all over the place.'

'Like she'd had a fit?' asked Richenda. 'Some people do have them. Especially when they are feeling under pressure.'

'I didn't think of that,' I said slowly. 'You mean it might have been a natural death?'

'The way I see it,' said Richenda, 'either this maid had a history of fits that we knew nothing about and she got herself so worked up about meeting you that it killed her or she did know something suspicious about the late Mrs Muller and someone killed her for it. The problem is that no one knew she was meeting you. If they'd known she had known something suspicious why hadn't she been dealt with before?' Richenda sighed. 'Sense would suggest she was stringing us along and it all got too much for her.'

'If she was prone to fits,' I said. 'And that is a

big if. We'll have to wait and see what the local doctor says.'

'Oh, Euphemia,' said Richenda, 'how can you be so naive. We're in the country. Muller is the biggest employer around here. He owns everything as far as the eye can see. The doctor will say whatever Muller tells him to.'

'And since there were rumours about his wife's death, whatever has happened you think he'll try and keep it quiet?'

'I would,' said Richenda honestly. 'Wouldn't you? No, don't answer that. I don't want to be made to feel guilty.'

'Then we're back where we started,' I said.

'Yes,' said Richenda, 'and it's almost time for dinner. We need to get back to the house and dress.'

'Are you serious?'

'Certainly, I need to show Muller I am a woman who can take everything in her stride.' The words 'unlike you' floated on the air. 'Besides, I want to hear the story from Bertram. He found her.'

By the time we returned to the house there was no sign of Lucy. A small car was parked to the side of the property and I assumed this was the doctor's vehicle. We made our way to our rooms without being accosted and changed for dinner. I chose something suitably sombre. Richenda, when I met her on the landing, was wearing a bright red dress. 'Too much?' she asked seeing my face.

'It is a little bright,' I said. 'I'm not convinced red is your best colour.'

Richenda bridled. 'When I need you to be my fashion consultant I will let you know. I'll have you know I went to a finishing school where we were taught about these things.' She gave my sombre dress a quick up and down. 'Appropriate for hired help,' she sniffed, and walked off ahead. This was the old Richenda I had come to not love. I sighed. One murder and the status quo swung back to the way it always had been.

We found Muller and Bertram having a quick pre-prandial drink in the drawing room. 'Mother didn't feel up to coming down tonight to dine,' explained Muller. 'It's so much harder to cope with disturbances like this when you are older, and she has had such a hard life.'

Bertram murmured something. I deliberately didn't listen hard enough to hear; as a man whose father had been murdered, who'd lost a step-sister before he'd even met her, had had servants murdered and lost what he erroneously thought of as the love of his life not that long ago. I suspected he had something to say about what constituted a hard life. And, of course, I'd been involved with every single one of those incidents. I decided the sherry glass Muller had passed me was quite fascinating. Meanwhile Richenda blundered in. 'Of course, poor old thing,' she said heartily. 'Slings and arrows and whatnots.'

'How kind of you to understand,' said Muller. 'I believe we are having turbot tonight. I do hope you all like it. Mrs Samson, our cook, has quite a way with it, but then I am biased. You will have to tell me what you think.'

'So you're restarting your autumn ball, Muller?' asked Bertram. 'Is that why I've been invited early – to help with the heavy lifting?'

'No,' said Muller, 'the flower arranging!'

And they both burst into laughter at some old joke that lay between them. I could see Richenda was bursting with curiosity, but she took her lead from Muller and told him that the invitations were coming on nicely. (She'd either been rummaging through my desk or was taking a shot in the dark that I was coming up to the mark.) 'Of course, if dear Mrs Muller is indisposed I would be more than willing to take on any extra tasks.'

Muller tut-tutted about not asking guests to help. 'But I have been a house guest so long I almost feel like...'

'One of the family?' finished Bertram cruelly. Richenda turned a deeper red than her dress. What with the colour of her hair, she resembled the inside of an overcooked rhubarb pie. Muller tactfully wandered over to the door to check if dinner was forthcoming.

'Honestly, Bertram, how could you?' Richenda was close to tears.

'If you're serious about Muller you need to show a bit more tact,' said Bertram brutally. 'He's not the kind of man to rise to the obvious. He will want a wife who can be diplomatic. Not someone who will go muscling in.'

'I was not! And I can be diplomatic,' said Richenda, stomping her foot.

'So I see,' said Bertram.

'Are none of you concerned about what happened to Lucy?' I asked quietly, so Muller wouldn't hear.

Both of them turned to me as one and said, 'Not before dinner, Euphemia!'

86

Muller came back from the doorway where he had been talking to a footman. 'It appears our dinner is ready. More like a little family supper really.' he smiled at Richenda, whose blush rose again. He turned to me. 'Euphemia, may I take you into dine? I'm sure Richenda and Bertram have a lot of catching up to do.'

And so it was I walked into dinner on Muller's arm with Richenda looking daggers at my back. Muller made a fuss of seating me next to him and seeing that I was given a glass of cool and light wine. Then a first course of mussels in yet more wine arrived and we were suddenly busy with attempting to eat the inside of the shells in a delicate manner. When I had worked at White Orchards I had seen Bertram more than once pick up the shells and suck the mussels out when he was dining alone. Tonight he fiddled with a tiny fork that looked ridiculous in his big hands. He sighed occasionally, and I knew he was wishing us all to the devil so he could tuck in. He loved seafood.

Richenda coped with the fork, but dribbled sauce down her front. I saw Muller looking at her askance from under his eyebrows. He did not appear impressed. Instead he kept up a flow of small talk with me, asking me about my upbringing in the vicarage and comparing it with life here on his estate. Obvious parallels between my youth and the youth of his wife came up despite my best efforts to sidestep them. By the time we reached the turbot both Bertram and Richenda were sending me glances that didn't bode well for a friendly after-dinner game of bridge. Or indeed any form of future harmony. Muller rose above all the discord by simply refusing to see it.

Later, after a dessert of cream, raspberries, and toasted oats, something Scotch I believe and therefore a little odd, we did play bridge. We cut cards for partners, but unfortunately I ended up paired with Muller. We beat the other two soundly, not least because they began to argue much as they must have done in the nursery, blaming the bad play on each other. Richenda did not appear to advantage.

When the game was finished Richenda and Bertram fell into a detailed and argumentative discussion of how each of them should have played better. Muller drew me aside. 'Shall we leave them to it?' he asked. 'I have no siblings, but I have often observed how fiercely they can quarrel one minute and yet be best of friends the next.'

'It would seem better to withdraw,' I said. 'I am quite tired. I think I shall retire to my room to read.'

'You are a very smart young woman,' said Muller. 'So many modern women think little beyond fashion and dances.'

'I could be going to read a fashion magazine,' I said.

'I think not.' Muller tapped me lightly on the arm. 'It is lovely night outside, clear and bright and not yet too cold. Would you do me the honour of taking a short walk with me in the gardens?'

His request startled me and it must have shown in my face. 'It is the only place we can talk where I am certain we will not be overheard,' said Muller. 'I promise to behave like a gentleman.'

'I would expect nothing less,' I said promptly,

though my immediate fear had been that this was an ungentlemanly proposal.

'My dear Euphemia,' said Muller lowering his voice, 'believe me, if I was intending to suggest anything improper it would be in a garden on a sunny afternoon, or at least a warm summer evening. Though the sun is about to set and we do get spectacular sunsets here.' Then he chuckled. 'It is unkind of me to tease. I give you my word I only want to talk to you. Will you come?'

I could hardly see how I could refuse. My mother would have known how to get herself out of this situation, but my experience since I had left home had been largely below stairs and I was no match for Muller.

We slipped away from the others, who appeared to be now arguing about the ownership of a long-deceased family pet. 'They will not miss us,' said Muller. He helped me into my wrap rather than calling a servant and led me through a side-door I hadn't noticed before out into the rose garden.

Twilight had fallen. The scent of roses was heavy in the air. Muller took me down a path and there suddenly in front of us was a bright orange sun, huge on the horizon, sinking below a distant line of trees. The sky was a dazzling mixture dappled with pink, purple and gold.

'Beautiful,' I said involuntarily.

'Indeed,' said Muller. 'This is why I work so hard in the city, so I can come home to this.'

'You have built a very lovely estate.'

'It functions well too,' said Muller. 'Forgive me if I sound proud, but unlike the Staplefords and Tip-tons of this world I did not start with advantages.'

'You were educated beside them.'

Muller nodded. 'It was thanks to a legacy from my godfather, but that was all I had – an education.'

'It has obviously stood you in good stead.'

'If I am honest it is as much about whom I met at school as what I learned,' said Muller. 'I am a self-made man. I think that is why I admire you so much. You started as a housemaid and here you are, companion to the lady of the house.'

I gave him a quizzical look. Richenda wasn't yet lady of this house. Muller continued to stare at the setting sun. He had a nice profile, no beard. Since kissing Rory it has occurred to me that kissing a man with a beard might be unpleasant. Especially if he wasn't scrupulous in keeping it clean. The taste of old soup would ruin a moment of romance. Never mind the prickles. But Muller was speaking again, 'My mother has taken to you very much. She has been suggesting certain options to me.' He turned to look at me. 'Has she spoken to you?'

'No more than to discuss matters concerning your ball.'

Muller nodded and made an affirmative noise in the back of his throat. 'She said you were proving especially adapt at managing invites and even seating plans. She said you knew the rules of social etiquette better than her.' He gave me a wry smile. 'You have no idea how much it will have cost her to make such an admission!'

'I haven't embarrassed her in any way, have I?' I asked, appalled. I could think of no other reason for this quiet word in the garden. 'I have always found her enormously welcoming and kind and I would hate to think...'

Muller half turned to me and placed a hand briefly on my shoulder. 'Euphemia, you can do no wrong in her eyes and I'm rather afraid that is becoming the problem.'

'I don't understand.'

'Of course not,' he said kindly. 'I never thought for a moment that you did.' He paused, 'But I fear that in time you would be unable to miss my mother's implications. She is not – er – subtle.' He took a deep breath, 'My mother's inclination, which I must stress is not mine, is that you would make her an excellent daughter-in-law.'

I was grateful for the glow of the setting sun. 'I see,' I said tightly.

'I do not think you have suggested this to her in any way,' said Muller quickly. 'I think you are completely blameless in this whole situation.'

'I have certainly never sought to...'

'Oh blast it, Euphemia!' Muller said abruptly. 'If it weren't for other circumstances I'd leap at her suggestion.'

'I'm a servant,' I said quietly.

'I don't bloody care,' exploded Muller. He walked a pace or two away from me. Stood as if collecting himself and then returned. 'Please let me apologise for my language,' he said.

'I've heard worse.'

'Well, you shouldn't have,' said Muller. 'Richard Stapleford is a cad.'

I nodded, feeling completely out of my depth.

'It has been my mother's dream as it was my father's to establish this estate. My parents as you know lived in Germany when I was younger. My father was German and my mother, despite her proper English Christian name, is half-German. It was important to them that I became an English gentleman.'

'Why?' I asked.

'Do you know,' said Muller with a chuckle, 'I'm not entirely sure. It has been a lifelong project for them and I have been raised as such and am comfortable as such. But as I said I do not come from money. I am a director of a bank: like many others I have made a good living this way.'

'You built this estate,' I said.

'And it is beginning to pay its way, but my capital is running short.'

I looked at the ground. I wished I was anywhere else.

'I have four hundred people relying on me for support as well as my tenants and farmers. I have a duty to the estate.'

I hazarded a guess that in other circumstances I would not have dared voice, 'Richenda's shares.'

'And her inheritance,' said Muller glumly. 'Please don't think too harshly of me. Richenda has made it clear she is eager to be established away from her brother. I am fond of her. She can be quite witty at times.'

'Yes, she can,' I said thoughtfully.

'She didn't have a hard life in the sense that many people do, but I think she was brought up in circumstances that did not allow her to become the best she could be. I think here, with me, she will be able to, well, mellow. I will offer affection, security, children I hope, and nothing less than respect at all times.'

'I take it you would like me to resign,' I said.

'No!' said Muller. He ran his hands through his immaculate hair. It curled attractively around his face. 'I don't. The last thing I want to take from you is the livelihood you have worked so hard to make for yourself. You support your family, as well, don't you?'

I nodded. We were in very dangerous waters.

'I know I'm making a mess of all this. I wanted to tell you I will be making a formal offer of marriage to Richenda at the ball.'

'Sir, you mustn't tell me this! Especially not before you tell my mistress!'

'I know I shouldn't, but I need you to understand something. Should Richenda accept me – and I think she will…'

Probably leap into your arms, I thought sourly, I hope you can take the weight.

'I will from then on regard you as Richenda's sister. You will always have a place in my home and I will not under any circumstances seek to take advantage of your position.' Even in the sunset I could see he was blushing. 'I will always behave towards you in a gentlemanly way.'

Neither of us said anything for a few moments.

'I'm not saying,' said Muller, 'that I am or will be a saint. Few married men are in my experience, but you will never, ever have anything to fear from me. I give you my word.'

I thought for one awful, and I blush to admit a delightful, moment that he might try and kiss me. But then I realised his very speech had precluded that option. 'We should get back,' I said.

'We will be missed.'

'Yes. I am deeply sorry I had to have this conversation with you at all, Euphemia, but my mother...' he trailed off.

'You should meet mine,' I said, trying to lighten the mood. 'On her best days she could be described as formidable.'

Muller laughed. 'I should be grateful. These gardens are entirely my mother's work. She and Bennie used to be out here everyday whatever the weather. I was forced to build the man a cottage near the main house, so she could consult him more easily.' He paused for a moment. 'This garden is her life's work, but...'

'She would prefer grandchildren,' I said.

'You are a very perceptive young lady.'

We made our way back to the house. He made me take his arm, so I wouldn't stumble in the dark. I had not now or ever any wish to marry him, but to think I had won a small part of his affections gave me a warm glow inside. He was a very charming man.

It was only when my head hit the pillow that night that I realised no one had raised the subject of Lucy's death. And that Muller's romantic intervention had driven any thoughts of Lucy completely out of my head.

Chapter Twelve

A Fall Before The Ball

Preparations for the ball continued apace and the weeks flew by.

After my late-night chat with Muller I became acutely aware that Mrs Muller did go out of her way to be nice to me. Richenda remained completely ignorant of this. Mrs Muller was frequently abrupt with her, but she had no way of knowing that Richenda's stepmother and even her own father had treated her far worse. In fact Richenda found Mrs Muller's abrupt little ways with her enchanting. 'She treats me like a member of the family,' she confided in me. 'No extra fuss like one would with a guest. She always comes straight to the point.'

I made appropriate noises when she was extolling how well she got on with Mrs Muller and changed the subject as quickly as possible. Richenda also took to asking me if I thought Muller was coming round to her. To which question I always replied cautiously in the affirmative and attempted to control her wardrobe choices.

Morally, I felt uncertain. Should I be helping her to a potentially loveless marriage? I turned that conversation in the garden over and over in my mind. By promising me a home and an income, Muller had effectively brought me in on his side, but it hadn't felt like that. It had genuinely felt that he was trying to do his best by me. I felt his honesty that night very deeply. One morning, a week before the ball, I took my livelihood in my hands and attempted to have a straight conversation with Richenda. She was looking over my plans for seating at the ball in the morning room. Bertram was away with Muller. It had become their usual practice to spend the day together if Muller was working on the estate – I think Bertram was trying to pick up tips from a successful enterprise and I encouraged this where I could. Goodness knew Bertram's estate, White Orchards, needed all the help it could get. On days Muller went into the city Bertram often spent time shadowing the estate factor. In fact, we had spent very little time in each other's company. Certainly there had been no opportunity given for me to raise the subject of the dead maid with him, and Bertram seemed all too eager to forget the entire matter. But it still worried me.

On this morning Richenda started as she often did, 'Do you think Muller values my opinion?' she asked. 'Only I suggested a colour scheme for the ball and I don't believe he is using it.'

'Mrs Muller chose the colour scheme,' I answered tactfully. Richenda's idea had involved orange, red, and green.

'Oh, I see. Maybe she didn't want to repeat a previous scheme?' said Richenda. 'We don't want the ball to bring back unpleasant memories.'

'They might be pleasant ones,' I said without thinking, as I considered sitting a bishop by a local curate for entertainment's sake. Bishops tend to ignore curates generally, but in public they must be seen to be Christian-like. As must the average curate, who generally thinks a bishop knows nothing about a working parish.

Richenda tapped me sharply on the arm. 'Do you think he is over his late wife?' she asked. 'For some reason the man seems to confide in you!'

This was as unwarranted as it was unfair. Since our rose garden conversation Muller and I had both made an effort to spend as little time alone as possible. I started to protest that he didn't confide in me, but my conscience wouldn't let me. Instead I said, 'I think he is devoted to this estate and wants to establish a family line.'

Richenda got up and started pacing. 'I know I don't have a skinny figure like some debutantes.'

I bit my lip. It was pushing it for Richenda to consider herself a debutante at her age. I doubted she had even been presented at the Royal Court. 'But I do have good childbearing hips. I'm not a frail little thing like his late wife.'

'That is very true,' I said, 'but I don't think it would be tactful to point that out.'

'Of course not,' said Richenda, 'I'm only talking to you. I need to believe I have a chance.'

'I'm sure you do,' I said. Richenda was almost pathetically grateful for my affirmation.

'And I've ordered a wonderful dress for the ball,' she stopped. 'Oh heavens, Euphemia, what will you wear? I never thought!'

'Am I invited?' I asked, surprised.

'Of course,' said Richenda, startling me with a peck on the cheek, 'I don't know what I would do without you.'

She said this with genuine gratitude, so why did it make me feel so guilty?

'I'm going to take coffee in Mrs Muller's room!' announced Richenda. I nodded, wondering if Mrs Muller knew anything about this. I got back on with my task. We had had replies now from almost everyone. Mrs Muller had asked me to invite that earl's daughter, but with rare tact my mother had declined. I was alarmed she had prolonged her stay with the canon and even more so that Mrs Muller was keeping in touch. Richenda hadn't mentioned her again. Happily, my mother had more sense than to write to me here. Doubtless prolonged contact with the dull and unambitious canon had reminded her how necessary my income was. But then why was she still here? I hoped she was not also entertaining thoughts of a loveless marriage. Although to be fair to Richenda I think she was quite struck by Muller. But I think she also knew she was never going to be love of his life.

And so the days wore on. With help from the seamstress Muller employed, I managed to adapt one of my dresses to something vaguely resembling a ball gown. It would be plain, simple, and darker than most of the other dresses there, but would also signify tactfully that I was not on an equal footing with the other ladies present. I had no jewellery to wear and this more than anything would indicate I was a servant. I didn't mind. I knew I was pretty, but I didn't want to draw attention to myself for many reasons. Though I did wonder if Bertram would dance with me. Since his arrival and the incident of the dead maid we had spoken even less than Muller and I had. If Bertram found me alone in a room he simply turned and left without a word. I confess I found this a little hurtful.

Then two days before the ball disaster struck. Mrs Muller, the housekeeper and the cook were working hard to finish off the preparations for the ball, but these were of so personal a nature – as this was a long-standing family ball – that I deliberately excluded myself from much of them. Of course if I was asked I offered an opinion or did what I was bid, but I tried hard to simply not be in the right place at the right time to be asked. I had successfully evaded Mrs Muller with a handful of flowers in the hall. I knew she wanted to ask me about the ball's colour scheme and as she had wisely refused Richenda's ideas (honestly I often wondered if Richenda is colour-blind) I felt it would be hugely tactless for me to offer an opinion. I was thus sitting reading quietly and contentedly in my room when I heard the scream.

I dropped my book and ran. The screams continued, leading me downstairs and to the front hall of the house. Muller stood there, having emerged from his study, an expression of concern and confusion on his face.

'Are you all right, Euphemia?' he asked with obvious concern.

'It wasn't me that screamed.' I replied.

Another scream came. It sounded fainter now. 'I do believe it is coming from outside,' said Muller.

'I had my window open,' I said. 'That would explain why it sounded so near.

'Wait here, my dear,' said Muller. 'I will go and investigate.' Of late he had taken pains to address as nothing but Miss St John. He was genuinely flustered.

'I think I should come with you,' I said. 'It sounds like a woman in distress and as such it may not be a gentleman's company she needs.'

'Of course, you're right,' said Muller. 'I only hope this will not involve you in further unpleasantness.' He opened the front door for me and we left the house. The first person we encountered was a small and rather grubby garden boy. 'What is happening?' demanded Muller.

'Some woman be screaming, sir,' said the child. In other circumstances I might have laughed.

'Where?' demanded Muller.

The child looked bemused. 'In the gardens, sir.'

'I think we need to go and look for ourselves,' I said.

Muller gave the child a frustrated look. Richard would have clipped his ear. Then he took my arm and led off at a smart pace to the rear gardens. There had been no more screams.

'It can't be that far,' I said, panting slightly.

'I don't know, Euphemia,' said Muller. 'Sound can carry in open countryside like you wouldn't believe.' There were beads of sweat on his forehead. I knew this must be reminding him of what had happened with his wife. I was almost absolutely certain that whatever was transpiring it was nothing to do with him. However charming Muller could be on demand, his distress at this time was obvious. We turned a corner and ran straight into Bertram.

'It's Richenda,' he panted. He bent over to catch his breath.

'Oh, dear God,' said Muller, turning a sickly shade of white.

Bertram straightened. 'Oh it's nothing like that, old chap. That silly mare of a half-sister of mine has only gone and fallen into a pile of poison ivy! Very painful, but far from fatal!'

'But the ball!' I exclaimed. Muller and I exchanged glances.

'Oh, she'll be better by then,' said Bertram assuredly.

'I think we should telephone the doctor,' I said.

'I agree,' said Muller. 'Perhaps you could help Bertram bring Richenda back to the house if she is otherwise unhurt. I doubt she would like me to see her.'

'Why?' said Bertram.

'Certainly,' I said and, tugging Bertram's sleeve, I told him to show me where Richenda lay.

When we found Richenda her skin had already started to show a reaction.

'Oh, Euphemia,' she wailed. 'Will it go down by the ball?'

'Muller has gone to fetch a doctor,' I said, avoiding the question.

Richenda looked down at her blotchy red hands. 'I can't see him like this. I can't!'

'I'm sure he's seen the effects of poison ivy before,' said Bertram. 'It's not like you're covered in blood or anything. Though you are rather bumpy!'

Richenda wailed again. I 'accidentally' kicked Bertram as I took Richenda's arm. She had half struggled out of the bushes so I could manage to help her without touching the ivy. Bertram waited until she was totally clear to offer his arm.

'How did it happen?' I asked.

'I have no idea,' said Richenda. 'Mrs Muller suggested I took a walk in the garden to get inspiration and to get some blooms. She still hasn't decided on the floral displays. I came round the corner and suddenly something or someone hit me full force in the back and I toppled face forward into the ivy.'

'Which was when you screamed,' said Bertram helpfully.

'I knew what it was even before it began to itch,' said Richenda. 'Why on earth has it not been removed from the garden? Even Richard's gardener wouldn't be so slack as to let it grow.'

'This is the wilderness garden,' said Bertram. 'Muller keeps it for his bees. He says it helps improve their honey yield.'

'Idiotic idea,' snapped Richenda. 'Everyone knows nature needs to be tamed.' She unhooked her arm from mine and scratched heartily at her forearm. I recaptured it.

'Stop it, Richenda! You'll only make it worse.'

'Oh, God,' cried Richenda, 'but it itches.'

'I'm sure the doctor will have something to help,' I said.

Mrs Muller appeared on the scene accompanied by Bennie. 'Oh dear,' said the head gardener, 'this doesn't look good.'

'What do you mean by having such plants in your garden?' demanded Richenda.

'It is a very pretty thing,' countered Mrs Muller.

'People don't regularly go jumping into the plants, miss,' said Bennie, removing his hat.

'You imbecile,' shouted Richenda. 'I should

have been warned. I was only fetching the flowers as Mrs Muller requested.'

'Oh, my dear,' said the lady, 'I never meant you to get them yourself. Bennie cuts all our flowers. As I am sure I explained to you.'

'But you told me exactly where they were!'

'Only because I could not remember their name,' said Mrs Muller. 'It was so you could tell Bennie the exact flowers I needed.'

Richenda gritted her teeth. 'Get me into the house,' she ordered Bertram and me.

When we were further away, Richenda muttered, 'I don't care what she says, she told me to get the wretched things. How was I meant to know she meant I was meant to ask Bennie? I'd never even met the man before.'

However, by the time the doctor arrived, despite my protests Richenda had managed to scratch herself so badly that the reaction had become red, raw, and most pronounced.

'It is a shame you weren't able to exercise a little more self-restraint, young lady,' said the doctor. 'I am afraid your body has reacted very badly to the poison.'

'I'm not going to die, am I?' said Richenda starting up off her day-bed in alarm.

The doctor laughed. 'Oh no, nothing like that. But I'm rather afraid you will be red and sore for the better part of a week.'

'I wish I was dead,' wailed Richenda.

'If I could have a word with you, Miss St John,' said the doctor. We left Richenda's room. I took him down to the morning room, which had become very much my working domain.

'I don't think your mistress will be going to the ball,' said the doctor bluntly. 'No self-control. I can leave you some salts you can use in her bath water to ease the itching – tepid water, mind. But other than that time will have to be the healer. If you can persuade her to refrain from scratching even more then it would be good. There's always the risk that any of the skin that breaks open can lead to infection and I don't need to tell you that can be fatal. It's imperative that she keeps clean and has fresh cloths on any exposed skin. If she finds it helps with the itching you can dampen them with cold water, but you will need to take care she doesn't catch a chill.'

Muller came into the room halfway through the doctor's instructions. 'You appear to be under a misconception, doctor,' he said. 'Miss St John is not a nurse. I will need you to provide us with one.'

'Oh, well,' said the doctor awkwardly, 'I naturally assumed that as a paid companion she would be the one to attend her mistress.'

Muller glared at him. 'You assumed wrongly.'

'Of course. Of course. My apologies, Miss St John. I will arrange for a nurse to be sent up to the house as quickly as possible, Mr Muller.'

Muller nodded curtly and left the room.

'Sorry, my dear,' said the doctor to me, 'I didn't realise you had such standing in the house or I'd have never...' he trailed off. It struck me then that he assumed I was Muller's mistress. I didn't blush simply because the idea confounded me so much. Instead, with unusual quickness of thought even for me, I took advantage of the situation and asked him about Lucy's death.

'No one here wishes to remember,' I finished.

'Unhappy memories and all that,' said the doctor. 'She simply had a fit. Choked on her own tongue.'

'Was she known for having fits?' I asked curiously.

'No,' admitted the doctor, 'but it is not uncommon for them to happen to young, excitable girls.'

This sounded like the kind of nonsense that doctor at the asylum had spouted, but I knew better than to challenge a medical man on his own ground. Especially a medical man who had the backing of the master of the house.

'Anyway,' he said as I saw him to the door, 'best if it's all forgotten now, what? The estate is finally getting on its feet. The autumn ball restored. It's quite like old times.'

Chapter Thirteen

The Lady Shall Go To The Ball

The morning of the ball Richenda insisted I send for the doctor. I knew from the state of her reddened face and the state of her skin that there would be little he could do. Nevertheless he was summoned and gave, as I expected, no hope for her attending the ball. You shouldn't have scratched so much,' he said sourly as if scolding a naughty child.

'I have a very sensitive skin,' shouted Richenda. 'I am a very sensitive person. If I cannot go to the ball it will make me ill!'

'You are ill,' said the doctor, throwing the nurse, who was backing quietly into the corner, a commiserating look. 'You cannot attend.'

'I want to go,' Richenda screamed.

'If you do not only will you make yourself very ill, but everyone will think you a freak,' said the doctor directly. He grabbed a small mirror off the dressing table. 'Have you looked at yourself?'

Richenda took one look and burst into tears. I left her to the nurse's ministrations. I was certain that no matter what I said or did I could not make anything better. That I knew Muller had intended proposing tonight made matters much worse.

Muller exited his room and met me on the landing. 'I heard the commotion,' he said. 'I assume Richenda is a little upset.'

'She is deeply disappointed.'

'Do you think she appreciates that it was impossible for me to cancel the ball? If we had already been engaged it would be different, but it would cause the very kind of talk I am trying to avoid.'

'On reflection I am sure she will understand. She is in a lot of discomfort,' I finished lamely.

'Should I visit her? Mother suggested I could if you chaperoned her.'

I thought of the awful prospect Richenda currently presented. Her current temperament as much as her temporary disfigurement would repulse many a suitor. 'You could send her a note?' I suggested.

'Flowers?' asked Muller.

I wrinkled my nose trying not to smile. Muller's eyes twinkled at me. 'No, maybe not appropriate. Chocolates? Cake?'

'Definitely cake.'

'I am afraid she will hear the ball up here. Music does echo through the house. Has she asked you to stay with her?'

I shook my head. 'I expected her to, but I don't think she wants anyone to see her as she is.'

'Good. I'm glad. I'm looking forward to dancing with you at the ball,' said Muller. 'Are you heading downstairs? Allow me to escort you.'

We found Mrs Muller at the bottom of the stairs who greeted us both ecstatically. 'The ballroom, it looks beautiful, Hans! Euphemia has been most helpful with the flowers and her seating plan! A masterpiece of diplomacy, tact, and entertainment. I know it is going to be a wonderful night!' She reached out a hand to me. 'Thank you, Liebling, you have been invaluable. We are very lucky to have you here. But after luncheon you must rest. We will dance until tomorrow, yes?'

'I am sure the ball will be a great success, Mrs Muller...'

'Tush. Tush. How many times have I told you, you must call me Philomena. After you have rested, but before we dress you must come to my room. I have a little something for you as a thank you for all your hard work.'

I blushed furiously. 'That is not necessary.'

'It is,' interrupted Mrs Muller. 'My Hans is happy. He is happy for the first time in years and you have helped to make it so. You will come and see me or I will be very cross. It is nothing. A trifle that will not embarrass you.' And with that she whirled off shouting for the cook.

'Oh dear,' said Muller, 'I did say she was very taken with you.'

I stammered something inarticulate.

'If it's anything outrageous call me. I'll sort her out.'

'Do you think it will be?'

Muller shook her head. 'Probably a brooch from some long-deceased great-aunt.'

'I couldn't possibly accept any such thing,' I exclaimed horrified.

'If it's anything like any of the other jewellery my mother inherited it will be ghastly and not worth very much. I will need to apologise to you for having to wear it.'

'What will you have to apologise for?' demanded Bertram appearing from the library. He frowned heavily.

'My mother is determined to give Euphemia a small present to thank her for her help in preparing for the ball.'

'Oh,' said Bertram, 'that's rather nice.' The frown deepened.

'I was warning Euphemia it will probably be some ghastly old bauble-ball.'

I blushed. Bertram's eyebrows raised. 'If you don't mind I'd like a quick word with Miss St John before luncheon.'

'Of course,' said Muller releasing my arm. 'I need to go and check that the stabling and motor car parking arrangements have been made properly – and separately!'

Bertram opened the library door and ushered

me in. 'You don't have any jewels to wear for the ball, do you?'

I blinked at him. 'You don't speak to me for weeks and this is the first thing you say?'

'What do you mean I haven't spoken to you? I speak to you all the time at meals, in the drawing room.'

'I meant alone.'

'I'm here to protect reputations, not break them,' said Bertram, scowling.

'Don't pull faces like that. It makes you look like an owl that's swallowed a beetle.'

'Owls don't eat beetles.'

'That's what I meant. An owl wouldn't like to eat a beetle.'

'Mice. Voles. Shrews.'

'And beetles by accident.'

'Euphemia, stop being so maddening!'

'A nocturnal avian's dietary requirements are hardly my fault,' I protested.

'You know what I mean.'

I sighed. 'Of course I don't have any jewels, but I will be dressed appropriately sombrely, so people will realise my status. Or do you think I shouldn't go if Richenda isn't attending?'

'I think you damn well deserve to go,' said Bertram. 'Besides, I was hoping to dance with you. You do know how to dance, don't you?'

'Of course. My mother ensured that I could.'

'I must meet this mother of yours one day. She sounds formidable.'

'Indeed,' I said.

'What does she do now? I know you support your family, but does she also work. Is she a cook?'

I almost choked with laughter at the thought of my mother in the kitchen. 'No, she teaches piano-forte.'

The luncheon gong sounded. I opened the library door. Bertram caught my arm. 'You know you can rely on me, don't you, Euphemia,' he said.

'Of course,' I answered tactfully, but only because I did not want to start another argument.

'By the way, did we ever find out who pushed Richenda into the bushes?'

'No,' I said, 'Muller thinks it must have been one of the garden boys racing around and too ashamed to admit it in case he was sacked.'

'Did we ever find out what happened to that house maid?'

'Choked on her own tongue during a fit, so the doctor says. Why are you asking all this now?'

'Oh, nothing,' said Bertram.

'Tell me,' I demanded, blocking the way.

'If you must know,' said Bertram scowling again, 'I have a very bad feeling about tonight.'

Chapter Fourteen

An Eventful Ball Begins

Mrs Muller spoke enough for all of us during luncheon. I escaped to my room to lie down with my head aching. I hadn't intended to sleep, but the light through the window had become grey before I knew it. I sat up feeling a little groggy with thoughts of dead maids, miscreant garden boys, and Bertram's unfortunate premonition running through my mind.

I have had occasion to question whether spiritualism and prediction of the future is entirely nonsense, but try as I might I could not bring myself to believe that Bertram was in any way psychic. About as psychic as an old sock. I muttered to myself as I rose to turn up the gas-lamp. I saw the clock face and remembered my promise to visit Philomena Muller before dressing. I could only hope that she had not been waiting for me too long. I quickly pinned up my hair. Much of it had tumbled out while I was resting. I would need to brush and re-do before the dinner and the ball, but I made myself respectable.

Mrs Muller answered my knock at her door at once. 'Come in. Come in,' she cried. 'I thought you had forgotten.

'I am so sorry. I fell asleep.'

'Poor Liebling. You have been working too hard. No matter, I am dressed.' She twirled before me in a simple but extremely elegant green gown that flattered her figure. I had never seen her look so good. At the point of her décolletage she had pinned a large carved black brooch. I saw what Muller meant. It was truly horrible. However round her neck hung a number of gold and diamond necklaces, drawing attention to her pale skin.

'You look lovely,' I said sincerely.

Philomena Muller gave me a huge smile. 'I am not too old yet,' she said and gave me a roguish wink. 'Now you, you have had my son's seamstress make you a dress. How dare you?'

'I didn't think he would mind,' I said, astonished.

'Everyone will mind,' declared Mrs Muller, 'it is horrible. I have had another made up from your measurements.' And then rather like a conjurer she gestured in the air and her maid, who had been waiting to one side, came forward with a dress in her arms. She held it up and I gasped. Silk, and of a deep warm chestnut colour that would both show off my pale skin and increase the glow of my own chestnut curls, it was quite the loveliest thing I have ever seen.

'Oh my,' I said, 'I can't accept this.'

'It won't fit me,' said Mrs Muller. 'Don't be ungrateful, child. You will look lovely.'

'Thank you,' I said. 'It is extremely kind of you.'

'How the devil do I make these cufflinks stay in,' demanded Bertram. I looked around in confusion.

'It's nothing. I am dressed. I want to check the dinner settings and that Pilton hasn't been sampling the wine! My maid will draw you a bath and help you dress. You cannot possibly do all that hair on your own.'

'The trick,' said Muller, 'is to have them large enough to stay in place and not large enough to be vulgar.'

'Do you remember the great big amethysts Baggy used to wear? Made him look like a shop assistant out on the town. Poor old chap. I still struggle to think he topped himself.'

'I don't think he did,' replied Muller. 'I don't even think it was him who murdered your mother.'

'Don't expect we'll ever know now,' said Bertram. 'Think I'll take that other drink now, Muller.'

'To a pleasanter future,' said Muller, sounding a little drunk already.

'Indeed,' said Bertram.

I looked wildly around the room, but could not see them. Unless they were under the bed they definitely were not in here.

Mrs Muller laughed at my confusion. 'It is only the boys having a few drinks before dinner. Dutch courage! I don't believe either of them are natural dancers. Hopefully they will recover themselves over dinner.'

'But where?'

Mrs Muller gestured at the fireplace. 'They are in the morning room with a decanter. Hiding from the rest of the staff, no doubt!' She laughed. 'Sound carries in this house. I'm so used to it I block it out now. Now take the dress, my dear, and my maid, she is very good. She will make you look like a princess.'

I gave Mrs Muller an impulsive small hug. She patted me on the back, but seemed pleased. When I returned to my room I found a small box on my dressing table. When I opened it I found a choker length collar of creamy pearls. There was no note. Doubtless Mrs Muller had known I would have been unable to accept such an expensive gift. As I later clasped them around my neck and looked at my reflection in the mirror I found I had quite the opposite feeling about this ball to Bertram.

I enjoyed dinner. I sat between a jolly bishop and a local magistrate. We had a lively discussion about the morality of poaching in the country and what should be done about it. When the ice creams and jellies were brought in the bishop discovered one he had once had in Italy, Venice in fact, and the magistrate had also visited the same city. I was then treated to an in-depth description of the wonders of Venice. I had read about the city of course, but I remained unconvinced that the two of them weren't teasing me when they said everything was borne about by boat and that the houses had no land around them whatsoever. But whatever the truth of the matter they were most genial company and when we left the table I felt happier than I had done in a very long time.

Muller came up behind me and tapped me on the shoulder. He looked very serious. 'My mother would like you to form part of the greeting line,' he said.

'I can't do that,' I said appalled. 'It would give entirely the wrong impression.'

'Yes, it would. But she will ask you even though I have advised against it. I thought I should fore-warn you.'

'I think I have remembered something I left up-stairs.'

'And you must not be without it tonight,' said Muller. 'By the way, those pearls look lovely on you – and the dress! Let us say that I never realised Bertram had such a long tongue. He has been positively panting over you at dinner. You could do worse, you know.'

I left him in confusion unable to answer such a comment and fled upstairs. As long as I missed the first few guests I would be able to join the ball proper. No one would think of adding to a greeting line after it had begun. That Mrs Muller wanted me there showed her intentions very strongly. Even Muller on the point of proposing to Richenda would not have included her in the welcome party at the door.

The lighting had been lowered on the upper floor. No doubt to help persuade people not to explore the house without invitation. However, by now I knew my way blind-fold about the house. I flitted into the shadows, out of the sight I hoped of the match-making Mrs Muller.

The gas lights on the landing, turned down almost dangerously low, hissed in my ears like angry serpents. I don't trust the things, never have, so I moved quickly past them. More quickly than the shadows warranted. I had my hand out-stretched reaching for the door handle when I ran into someone. I started back, ready to apologise, but the figure pushed roughly past me. Too roughly. I over balanced and fell to the floor with an undignified squeak. As he, for the figure wore trousers, ran past a window, I saw only that he was of below average height.

I sat there for a moment catching my breath. I realise many young ladies would have been faint-ing or screaming by now, but in comparison with some of my previous encounters in the dark this episode struck me as comparatively mild. I checked the hem of my dress for pulls and ensured my heels did not catch as I stood. The episode didn't seem worth disturbing the ball for, but I felt I should tell someone. I went in search of Bertram.

I found him chatting to a very pretty and very young brunette. Bertram is not overly tall, but this girl could not match him in height. Instead she stood there, a large proportion of her milky skin spilling out of her outrageous evening gown, staring up at him with large brown, cow-like eyes.

'Mr Stapleford,' I said, 'I need to talk to you.'

'Oh Euphemia, allow me to introduce Miss Antonia Sims...'

'Very nice to meet you,' I said and tugged him away by his arm. The little cow-person stood alone looking forlorn.

'Euphemia, you can't do that it's so rude,' protested Bertram as I towed him from the room.

'I'm sure Miss Antonia will wait for you.'

'Not if she sees me being dragged off like prey to your lair.'

'Don't be ridiculous. I need you to come upstairs with me.'

'Euphemia!' expounded Bertram.

'Don't be an ass,' I responded, and this less than lover-like description seemed to convince him something was afoot.

'What have you done?' he asked.

'It's what's been done to me,' I said.

'Oh God,' said Bertram, as he followed me up the stairs, 'you haven't found another dead body, have you?'

'Not yet.'

'Not yet!'

'Come to the back of the landing away from the stairs. I don't want anyone to see us up here.'

'Euphemia, I am getting very confused,' said Bertram.

'Oh, for heaven's sake, shut up and let me explain.'

'Gladly.' Bertram scowled fiercely.

'Muller asked me to escape from the party for a little while as his mother wanted to include me in the welcome line-up.'

'Dash it, Euphemia, it's not done to steal a bridegroom from my sister. Even if she is repulsive at times.'

'Stop dashing me and listen. Neither Muller or I have any designs on the other. We both know Mrs Muller's intentions and didn't want her to cause an embarrassing scene.'

'So you and Muller are in each other's confidence?' Bertram said this in a more puzzled than angry tone.

'To some extent,' I admitted, 'but not in any way that engages our affections. If anything I've been trying to help him and your sister get together.'

'Very good of you, I'm sure. Do you smell something funny?'

'There's nothing funny about it. It's all been totally above board,' I said. 'Richenda has admitted to me she wants to marry Muller. She knows he doesn't love her, but she thinks they would work well together.'

'Got to be better than her living with Richard. My stepbrother is a cad.'

'Gosh, I think maybe the encounter took more out of me than I thought. I need to sit down.' I slid down the wall. Bertram did the same so he could continue talking to me on my level.

'Encounter?'

'I came up here to get out of the way. It was dark and I was walking very quickly. I ran into someone.'

'Who?'

'I don't know. Someone short, wearing trousers. A man, I suppose. Goodness, do you think those oysters at dinner were fresh? I'm feeling a little unwell.'

'Me too,' said Bertram. 'Maybe we should stay up here till we feel better. Don't want to spoil the party.'

'Exactly,' I said, resting my head on his shoulder.

'So who did this man turn out to be?'

'No idea. He ran off down the corridor. I came to fetch you. I didn't want to make a fuss. It wasn't like that night I ran into Mrs Wilson's attacker.' I shivered.

'No, he gave you concussion.'

'Not a polite thing to do,' I agreed.

Bertram rubbed his eyes and shook his head. 'Where was this man?'

'Over there!' I pointed. It seemed difficult to get my arm steady. As I reached out a waving finger one of the gas lamps guttered and went out.

'Good god, Euphemia,' said Bertram. 'Get up! Get up!'

'I'm quite comfortable here.'

Bertram gave up pulling at my arm and got to his feet. He staggered from one foot to the other.

'Mrs Muller heard you drinking,' I said. 'Looks like you had a little too much.'

Bertram ignored me and lurched over to the nearest door. He threw it open and headed in. Moments later I heard the window being thrown up.

'Muller does have remarkably comfortable walls,' I said. My eyes were closing. I felt myself drifting peacefully on a quiet sea when a splash of cold water hit me in the face. Bertram stood above me with a tooth mug. 'Come on,' he said. He was no longer staggering. He pulled me to my feet. I didn't remember quite how they worked so he dragged me into Richenda's room. 'She looks like a punnet of cherries,' I said. Bertram shoved my head out the window.

Several lungfuls of air later I vomited down the side of Muller's house. 'Stay there,' said Bertram. 'Don't fall out.' He ran out of the room. I leaked more of what had been an excellent dinner down the wall. Around me I heard the sound of windows being thrown open. Another spasm overcame me and I gave my whole attention to emptying the rest of my stomach out of the window.

Chapter Fifteen

Murdcrous Intent

It seemed that I would be sick for ever, but eventually my stomach stopped heaving. Sweat beaded my forehead and my hair hung loose around my face. Bertram pulled me back into the room and gently wiped my face with a damp cloth. 'My poor Euphemia,' he said.

'Oysters,' I said apologetically.

'No,' said Bertram, 'gas. Your intruder turned down the lamps so low they were leaking poisonous fumes.'

I leant back, feeling terrible. 'What have I done this time?'

'Nothing,' said Bertram. 'Whoever it was, I think he was after Richenda. We're in her room.'

And on cue, Richenda leaned over and vomited onto the carpet.

Bertram helped me up. 'I think we'll get a maid to deal with that.'

The hall outside was now completely dark. I shivered with fear. 'No other way,' said Bertram. 'Until the gas clears I daren't turn on a lamp. I've turned them all off and the window in your room is wide open. Yours is furthest away from the leaking lamp, so you should be all right.'

'That one. It was outside Richenda's door?' I asked.

'Yes,' said Bertram, laying me down on a chaise longue by the window in my room. 'You should be fine. I'll summon the doctor in case.'

'But...'

'I'll say one of the new maids turned the lamps down dangerously low.'

'But the intruder might still be here.'

'He almost certainly is,' said Bertram. 'I'll tell Muller the truth and he can decide what to do. In the meantime I'll get maids to attend to both you and my sister. You won't be alone for a moment.' He rang the bell.

'But Richenda is,' I protested.

'I've got the doors open,' said Bertram. 'I can see you both.'

And with this reassurance I drifted off towards sleep. A cold breeze blew through the window on to my face. The scent from the garden at another time I would have found heavenly. Mrs Muller really had created a wonderful garden. I wondered why this bothered me so much, but before I could answer myself I had slipped into sleep.

As a first ball I can't say I did very much dancing. I became dimly aware of figures going in and out of my room. The doctor cursed the gas lamps and all servants. Bertram hovered by my side for a long time. Then Muller replaced him. He bent down to whisper to me. 'I had to assure myself you were safe. Stapleford will stay with you. Don't worry, I have everything under control. Rest now.' I sighed and decided to trust him. He really was such a charming man. My dreams were confused. Hollyhocks chased gas lamps in flat caps through a jungle. At the heart of the jungle roared a lion. It had the face of Richard Stapleford.

The next morning a maid came to help me wash and dress. I went down to breakfast to find a council of war awaiting me and at the centre of the breakfast table sat none other than Richard Stapleford, master of Stapleford Hall and my long-term adversary. As I entered he was indeed mid-roar.

'You!' I said as dramatically as any bad actress. Richard barely glanced at me.

Muller and Bertram were also present. There was no sign of Mrs Muller. Muller got up to pull out a chair for me. 'My mother sends her apologies,' he said. 'She is very distressed by what has happened and feels unable to join us.'

'I think that's for the best,' said Richard.

Muller ignored him. He set my chair for me. 'The doctor assures me you have taken no lasting ill, Miss St John. Bertram, ring for some fresh tea!'

'Damn the tea,' said Richard. He speared a rasher of bacon on his plate with unnecessary force. All three gentlemen had helped themselves to the breakfast buffet. Obviously, it was assumed that as a weak and frail female I would not be wanting more than tea this morning. I hated to admit it, but they were right.

'How is Richenda?' I asked. 'Why is he here?'

'Richenda is also recovering,' said Muller. 'Sir Richard gate-crashed our ball to ask his sister to return home.'

'It was you,' I said accusingly. 'You were the man at the window.'

'What is the wench talking about?' spat Richard. 'The gas has addled what wits she had.'

'I must ask you to keep a civil tongue in your head, sir,' said Muller. 'Miss St John is an invited guest in my house. You are not.'

'Got you too, has she?' said the detestable Richard. 'Don't know how she does it!'

Muller scrapped back his chair and stood. 'Now then, old man,' said Bertram uneasily.

'Isn't the most important thing that we work out who is trying to murder Richenda?' I interjected.

'What do you mean,' bellowed Richard.

'Only that she was meant to die last night.'

The room went very quiet. Finally Richard spoke, 'I swear if this is one your tricks, wench, I will…'

'Enough,' roared Muller. We all started. Everyone knew Muller never raised his voice. He was famous for it.

'Right, now I finally have your attention, I must

tell you I agree with Miss St John. I believe Richenda's life has been in jeopardy and continues to be so.'

'But who would harm me sister?' asked Richard, in more of a bleating than an angry tone.

'You,' said Bertram. 'On her death her share of our father's estate reverts to you.'

'I don't need the money,' snapped Richard.

'I don't know about that,' said Muller more quietly, 'but you certainly want her shares.' He sat down again.

'So do you,' snapped Richard.

'But I would not get them if she died,' said Muller.

'I think perhaps you had better leave, Euphemia,' said Bertram. 'You should leave us to work this out.'

'You mean leave the men to sort it out?' I said. 'I don't think so. While Richenda remains in bed I will be her representative.'

'I can represent my own damned sister,' said Richard.

'But that's exactly the point,' said Muller. 'You can't. Your motives are suspect.'

'Did you bring Barker with you?' I asked.

'What's my factor got to do with it?'

'You sent him here to threaten me to try and force Richenda to go back to Stapleford Hall.'

'I did no such thing,' said Richard. 'I told the damn man to present my compliments and explain I wanted Richenda home.'

'That isn't what he did,' I said. 'And he spread the most scurrilous rumours about Mr Muller.'

'He did?' said Muller startled. He frowned. 'It

123

was after this that I found you searching my attic.'

'The pigeon disturbed Richenda,' I said.

'And did she think?' asked Muller horrified.

'No, I'm sure she didn't,' I answered quickly. 'She has always believed in you.'

'As I suppose you have too,' said Richard softly.

I turned to face him straight on. 'What is that meant to mean?'

'Only that we might all be overlooking the one person you would genuinely benefit from Richenda's death.'

'Who?' I asked.

'You!' said Richard, pointing an eggy knife at me in a threatening manner. 'You've already got Muller half under your spell. I reckon you thought you'd have a fine life as Mrs Hans Muller!'

Neither Bertram nor Muller sprang immediately to my defence. I gave them both a hard look. Bertram dropped his gaze and Muller half shrugged an apology.

'You've made a career out of convincing respectable men you are better than you are,' continued Richard. 'You are a viper in any household.'

Bertram sat up straighter at that. 'Oh, I say, that's not on!'

'I must request you again to keep a civil tongue when you address my guest in my house,' said Muller firmly.

'Listen to you both,' exclaimed Richard. 'She's got you both wrapped around her little finger.'

'Entertaining as your suspicions may be,' I said reverting to my natural accent, my voice sharp as glass, 'they are merely a diversion from the real issue. It seems unlikely that even a weak-willed female would gas herself rather than her victim. Or manage to push Richenda into poison ivy while being with witnesses in the house.'

'You could have paid someone to do it,' snapped Richard.

'I am not the one with hired help on hand,' I replied.

'The poison ivy couldn't have killed her,' said Bertram, 'could it?'

'Probably not,' I said. 'The doctor did say there was always the danger of infection if a patient scratched the scabs.'

'Or of a worse reaction,' added Muller. 'I don't think whoever arranged for her to fall would have minded if she had died, but at the time I do not believe it was the main motive.'

'They wanted her not to go to the ball,' I said. Muller paled.

'You had a new dress,' he said.

'Your mother ordered it for me. I didn't know anything about it until last night.' I paused. 'She sent Richenda to fetch some blooms, but she claimed she had to give Richenda directions because she couldn't remember the name. But she designed the gardens. You said they were her life's work.'

'They are,' answered Muller, very quietly.

'Bennie has been with you a long time?' I asked.

'Yes. I know. He's not tall.'

'What has that got to do with anything?' snapped Richard.

But a deeper revelation had broken in on me. I spoke without thinking who was present. 'The chimney,' I said, 'she would have heard every word when I told Richenda that Lucy had offered to sell us information about the death of the late Mrs Muller.'

'Lucy said what?' gasped Muller.

'She said your valet had told her something.'

'What?' pressed Muller.

'I have no idea. She died before she could tell me.'

'The maid by the driveway?' said Bertram. 'Are you suggesting that...'

'Can a poisoning be made to look like a fit?'

'No.' Muller was shaking his head. 'If she was killed it would mean...'

'That there was a danger she knew something about the late Mrs Muller's death.'

Hans Muller sat there, ashen-faced, as if his world had fallen in around him.

'You fiend!' cried Bertram leaping to his feet. 'You lady-murderer... I mean, murderer of ladies... I mean– Fiend!'

Chapter Sixteen

Final Farewells

'She can't have known,' muttered Muller. He looked at me in appeal. 'He must have done it for her. Done what he thought she wanted.'

'Fiend!' cried Bertram again. Richard sat between the two men. 'Mad house,' he grunted. 'Bloody mad house.' He applied himself to his sausages and bacon once more.

I too rose, a little unsteadily. 'You have it wrong, Bertram,' I said and I could hear my voice shaking. 'Mr Muller is entirely innocent. If anyone here is at fault it is me.'

'No,' cried Muller. 'None of this is your fault.'

'But if I hadn't come here,' I begun.

'Told you it would be this wretched wench's fault,' said Richard as he decapitated a boiled egg. 'Now, won't you all sit down and explain to me exactly what Euphemia has done.'

Bertram sank slowly back into his seat, an expression of total bemusement on his face.

'You will have to excuse me one moment,' said Muller tightly, 'there is something I must check on.'

'I will go with you,' I said. Muller made as if to protest, but I cut him off. 'This is not something for you to do alone.'

'Should I telephone to the police?' asked Bertram, still confused but trying to join in.

'I suspect, unfortunately, that will not be necessary,' I said.

Further understanding dawned in Muller's eyes. Then he ran from the room. I followed as fast as my skirts would let me.

Even so, I met him on the landing as he closed his mother's door behind him. He clutched a note in his hand. He looked stunned.

'I am so sorry,' I said.

'Did you know that she would do this?' he asked in a low voice.

'No,' I said. 'The pieces only came together when we were talking now. Then I remembered

127

you had said she had declined to come down to breakfast. She knew we would work it out. She's gone, isn't she?'

Muller nodded. Then he took my wrist. His fingers were gentle but unyielding. 'Come with me. I must talk to you.' He pulled me along the landing and into his bedroom. He let me go as soon as we were inside, but he shut and locked the door. My heart began to beat a little faster. After all I had no proof my theories were right. In the centre of the room stood an enormous four poster bed, hung with green curtains. Muller dropped the door key in his waistcoat pocket and I began to feel even more uneasy.

'Can I see the letter?' I asked.

Muller shook his head, but held it out to me. 'It won't help you. She wrote in German.' I took it. He told the truth. None of the words held any meaning for me. Muller sank down on the edge of his bed. 'I think you had better tell me what you think is going on,' he said in a level voice.

'And if I don't?' I said.

'We will sit here a long time.'

'And if I do?'

'Then we can decide what to do.'

I hesitated.

'I am not going to hurt you, Euphemia, but I would very much prefer it if you would piece this puzzle together for me.'

'I can assume Mrs Muller is dead?'

He nodded.

'Does it matter then?' I asked. 'She's gone. Once Bennie is apprehended it will all be over.'

'My mother and her gardener were very close. I

doubt he will survive her.'

'Oh my God, you mean he too would take his own life? Then we must go to him. Prevent him.'

'No.' said Muller firmly. 'If he has chosen to take the gentleman's way out then that is for the best.'

'You would sit here while he might be dying?' I asked.

Muller nodded. 'Tell me what you think happened, Euphemia. I am driving myself mad with my thoughts.'

'I have no proof,' I said.

'Tell me!' shouted Muller.

I backed up against the door. 'It's every bit as bad as you fear,' I said quietly. 'You told me your mother loved her garden, but you didn't disagree when I said she would rather have grandchildren. It's a family obsession to continue the line.'

'But I was going to marry Richenda! She knew that!'

'For some reason she preferred me,' I said bluntly. I knew why, but I had no intention of telling him. 'I imagine she thought because I was younger I would be more likely to be able to have several children for you.' I took a deep breath. 'She arranged for Richenda to be pushed into the ivy by Bennie, so you would dance with me at the ball. I think you are right, that she hoped Richenda would become severely ill. When it became clear she was recovering, she sent Bennie to turn down the gas lamps so the fumes would overcome her.'

'He could have blown the whole house up!'

'If I hadn't disturbed him I think he would have stayed around to turn them up again. It may be he only intended for them to make her sleepy...'

'To prevent her coming down to the ball?' asked Muller.

'So he could more easily suffocate her in her sleep.'

'Dear God.' The look of devastation on his face was hard to see.

I moved away from the door. I took a chair and placed it opposite him. 'It gets worse.'

'Lucy?'

I nodded. 'Your mother's room is above the morning room. She heard Richenda and me making plans to pay Lucy for gossip.'

'And Bennie killed her too? She would have had nothing to tell you.'

'Obviously your mother thought otherwise,' I said carefully.

'Charlotte died from heart failure.'

'That isn't the whole truth, is it?' I said. 'What caused Charlotte, your beloved wife, who kept miscarrying your children, to suffer heart failure?'

Muller slumped. 'Angel's Trumpet. Those beautiful flowers on the pavilion. Shake several over a tea cup, stir and you will never wake up. She admits it in the letter. Claims it would have been a gentle death. It seems our local doctor is open to bribes. He has a son he wants to send to a good school. The ambition of parents,' said Muller bitterly. 'Did you guess?'

'Between them Bennie and your mother had a vast knowledge of plants and herbs, and that includes plants that are toxic. All gardeners must know these so the children, pets, and even the adults of the household do not come to harm.'

'My mother killed Charlotte because she

130

couldn't have children.'

'I feared so.'

Muller sat silently for some time. I waited. I knew I could not wrest the key from him. I did not know what he would do if I called for help. Had he been involved in his mother's schemes? Complicit? Now I had laid all I feared bare would he silence me too? I clenched my muscles and tried not to shake. I must not show fear.

Then Muller dropped his head in his hands and began to sob. My next action I will always claim was involuntary. I went to sit next to him and put my arms around him. He lent on me and wept like a child.

Finally he stopped. He wiped his face with his handkerchief, gently disengaging my arms. 'I am so sorry, Euphemia,' he said. 'Everything this family has put you through. It is too much. I will go and tell Bertram to telephone to the police now and send someone to Bennie's house. There may still be time.' He made to rise.

I put a hand on his shoulder, restraining him with my touch. 'No,' I said. 'We both know it is too late for the gardener by now. We have spent too much time here.'

'Your reputation!' said Muller.

'Was never that high with the Staplefords!' I gave a weak smile. 'Your mother and Bennie have paid for their actions with their lives. Nothing either of us can do will bring back either Charlotte or Lucy. Summoning the police will cause nothing but unpleasantness to all those involved.'

Before he could stop me I threw his mother's confession on the fire. 'If nothing else,' I said,

'Richenda would never forgive me if you let a constable interview her in the state she is currently in!'

'That damned doctor. Heart failure?'

'It is what we all die of eventually. It may be that he simply did not know or it is what he thought you also wanted him to put. I doubt he knew she was poisoned. Your mother probably told him to put something innocuous and he didn't ask any questions.'

'I would have wanted to know the truth.'

'Honestly? That your mother had conspired to take your wife from you?'

He nodded. 'It would have saved Lucy's life.'

'Well, now there is no one left to take account of.'

'Except me,' said Muller. 'I think I suspected Mother a long time ago. And then when she became so keen for me to marry you and bought you that amazing dress...'

Not to mention, I thought, she'd heard me admit in the morning room that I was the grand-daughter of an earl.

'I feared she had arranged Richenda's accident, and then when I had considered she might have done that I began to...'

'Fear more,' I finished for him. 'But it was too late by then.'

'How could I have been so blind,' raged Muller. 'I should have protected Charlotte. I loved her with all my heart.'

'I'm sure she knew that,' I said. 'I expect she never knew what happened to her.'

'You think so?' asked Muller hopefully.

'Heart failure is very sudden,' I said with no

knowledge whatsoever to back up my assumption. His face cleared a little.

'But what do we tell the others about Mother?'

'This is where your local doctor must once again prove his worth. School fees must be paid annually. Your mother was hardly elderly, but she was of an age when it is not uncommon for people to die. She had said she was feeling unwell.'

'But Bennie?'

'If we wait until your mother has been seen by the doctor, people will assume that he took his life as he was so devastated by your mother's death. They may draw some inappropriate conclusions...'

'I'm not sure they would be inappropriate,' said Muller almost savagely. 'He must have had a great regard for her to do her bidding.'

'Loyalty is prized among servants,' I said vaguely.

'As you have always been loyal to Richenda.' Muller frowned at me. 'You are very adapt at arranging these matters.'

'Living with the Staplefords has given me an insight to a world I would not otherwise have encountered.'

'Am I wrong to consider marrying Richenda? Is she also...'

'Versed in these ways? I think Richenda will improve vastly when she is away from Stapleford Hall and her brother.'

Muller nodded. 'Under the circumstances I could not reconsider offering my proposals to you. I could not ask you to join such a family.'

'But you can ask Richenda?'

'Richenda and I will make a bargain. We will

each get what we want from this union.'

'I think she is more than half in love with you,' I said.

Muller shrugged. 'I will always treat her kindly, you have my word. There will also always be a home for you here if you still wish it.'

I sighed. 'I have nowhere else to go,' I said simply.

'Then you should look, Euphemia,' said Hans Muller, 'and I say this to you as a friend.'

Chapter Seventeen

Stapleford Hall

There was, of course, quite a fuss when Muller and I finally exited his room. This was not helped by Bertram coming up the stairs as we exited and thus having a very good view of Muller and I together silhouetted against the backdrop of his enormous bed. I believe he would have rushed up and done his best to knock Muller down if Muller hadn't taken that exact moment to announce the death of his mother. It seems in the gentlemanly way of things you cannot knock down the recently bereaved. Bertram said all that was polite though clenched teeth while throwing both of us looks he clearly hoped would kill.

I left Muller to summon the doctor, the house-keeper and the staff necessary to oversee the sad events. I will tell Richenda everything, I said quietly to him as I slipped away. I was rewarded with a smile. 'Thank you,' he said. 'It is only fair she knows before I ask her. Don't tell her that though.' I shook my head. Bertram scowled furiously at us and I saw his fingers twitch over a fine tall vase. I was unsure which of us he most wanted to throw it at, so I made my escape to Richenda's room.

I told her everything she had missed and everything I had surmised. 'So there's no proof,' she said.

'None whatsoever.' I said.

'But Muller didn't contest any of it?'

'No.'

'Do you believe him?'

'I'm not sure what you mean?'

'Do you believe it was his mother who arranged all these deaths and not Muller himself?'

'If you want me to be honest,' I said slowly, 'it is not possible to rule that out, but I don't believe he did so.' I stressed the word 'believe'.

'You told me once before you almost succumbed to his charm.'

'Do I think this might have happened again?'

'That you might have been overwhelmed.'

'He is very charming,' I admitted. 'And frankly there is no way we can ever know the truth now.'

'I'd better make damn sure I give him a couple of bouncing babies as soon as possible after the wedding,' said Richenda.

I gave an uneasy smile.

With Muller in mourning there was no way we could stay on as guests in his house. Much to my surprise Richenda, heavily veiled, sent me to fetch Muller to her room. I did point out he had other things to do and we needed to make plans. 'I know that,' said Richenda. 'What do you think I'm doing?'

To my amazement Muller left his arrangements and came at once. I hovered outside her door when Muller went inside to lend some kind of respectability to proceedings. They spoke in low voices for long enough that I was afraid Bertram would come creeping up the stairs again to accuse me of improper behaviour. When the door did open, Muller came out smiling. 'You can congratulate me,' he whispered in my ear. He walked off with more spring in his step than I had seen for some time. He stopped at the top of the stairs. 'Could you stay with her a little longer, Euphemia? There is someone I am sending up for her to see.' I nodded. I thought he meant the doctor.

Richenda and I played cards for the next two hours. I tried to lose to her, so she wouldn't become too grumpy, but she was a very bad player. However, she lasted only ten minutes before she broke the news to me that she and Muller were now engaged. 'We'll have a proper celebration once this blasted rash has gone down,' she said. 'Though it won't be that big because of his mother's and Tippy's deaths. I do think the ballroom will look good in green and orange.' I felt a twinge of sympathy for Muller.

When Richenda's visitor did arrive he proved to be an unfamiliar man in an expensively discreet grey suit carrying a briefcase. He nodded at me. 'She'll do,' he said. 'But we'll need another one.'

'No,' said Richenda. 'Could you leave us, Euphemia and send up two maids. Two.'

I did as I was bid and then slowly made my way downstairs. Muller was nowhere in sight. I found Richard drinking heavily in the library and managed to withdraw before he saw me. I went out into the garden wondering if Bennie's fate had yet been discovered. Muller and I could have been wrong. He could have fled the scene.

As soon as I was outside I saw a number of servants and gardeners congregated around the head gardener's house, so it seemed we had been right. I was about to go back into the house and, frankly, hide in my room until anyone came to fetch me, when I walked into Bertram. He was strolling along the gravel drive, his hands in his pockets, kicking at the stones. He looked up and saw me.

'Don't know what to do,' he said. 'Do you think I should take off?'

'I think we all need to leave,' I said. 'But it's probably best that you don't leave before Richenda.'

'Even though Richard is here?'

'You'd be a real rat to run out and leave us alone with him,' I said.

Bertram grinned. 'It's still an appealing idea.' Then he dropped his head for a moment and looked up at me somewhat abashed. 'I'm sorry I thought you were ... earlier ... with Muller.'

'Bertram,' I said stoutly, 'if I ever decide to have a liaison with any man I will do it with discretion. You can be assured I will never rise from a crowded breakfast table and make my way to – to an indiscretion in public view!'

'Especially before you've eaten anything,' said Bertram smiling.

'You're incorrigible!'

We made our way back into the house once again in reasonable accord. 'I suggest we go to our rooms until summoned,' I said. 'Richard isn't going anywhere today. He's already drunk and it will take time to pack up Richenda's belongings.'

'But where are you – we – going?' asked Bertram.

'I have no idea. How is White Orchards?'

'Habitable,' said Bertram unencouragingly. 'Bit lacking in comfort at present.'

'It may have to do,' I said.

Bertram wandered away looking worried. I began to worry that habitable might not include a roof. However, my worries were set aside during a rather remarkable dinner. Luncheon having been sent up to our rooms on a tray and consisting of no more than a sandwich and a pot of tea, I was surprised to be told by a maid that we would be dressing for dinner that night.

I found something suitably dark and discreet – not difficult in a companion's wardrobe – and made my way down as soon as the dinner gong sounded. I found Bertram, Richard, Muller and a very veiled Richenda already having sherry in the library. 'Heavens,' I said to her, 'I didn't realise you were coming down. I would have come to help.'

Richenda waved my concerns aside. 'No, Hans and I felt it was important to tell you all our announcement as soon as possible. This has been such a sad day that we both felt it was appropriate to do something to lighten the darkness.'

Which I realised was a quaint way of trying to explain why they were not reacting to the rules of mourning as expected. Both of them wanted to secure their futures no matter how it looked.

'What announcement,' said Richard baffled.

'Your sister has done the honour of accepting my hand in marriage,' said Muller.

'She what!' roared Richard. I wondered if he had become a little deaf since I had last seen him. He was certainly roaring a lot.

'Congratulations,' said Bertram. 'I hope you will both be very happy.'

'Dammit! I'm the head of the family and I forbid it!'

'I'm of age, Richard. Or had you forgotten?'

'There's one other little matter we thought we should draw to the family's attention,' said Muller and he gave an embarrassed cough. 'Richenda and I thought...'

'That I should make a will,' said the lady in question. 'Everything that has happened recently has brought the whole issue of mortality to my mind.' She gave Richard a hard look. 'Hans arranged for a lawyer to come to me today, so it's been done correctly. When I am married should anything happen to me after I have married my money and shares go to Muller without reservation. However, should I die before I marry I have bequeathed all my money and shares to the home I set up for fallen women.'

There was a stunned silence. Then Bertram raised his glass and said, 'Hear, Hear!'

I joined in though I felt Richenda had been incautious. I guessed it was her way of showing

Muller she trusted him completely. I could only hope she was right.

When we had all drunk their health, Richenda spoke again. 'I have one more matter to announce. Obviously I cannot stay here while I prepare for my marriage. Therefore I will be returning, as is my right, to Stapleford Hall. Euphemia will accompany me, as I hope will you, Bertram.' She bestowed a loving smile on her stepbrother and a less sweet one on her twin.

'Now that is all cleared up,' said Muller, 'can I suggest we go in to dine. I, for one, have found this an exceedingly long day.'

Bertram took my arm and Muller took Richenda's. Richard stayed where he was, open-mouthed, clearly floored, and bemused by what had just happened. I knew his silence would not last for long. There would doubtless be shouting over the soup, tantrums over the fish and melees over the entree, but the more I thought about what Richenda had done the better I thought of her plan. Richard would gain nothing by harming her. Instead he could lose all hope of ever winning back those shares. His best option now, as Barker would no doubt point out to him, would be to try and sweet talk his way back into Richenda's good books. He would doubtless try to talk her out of the marriage and I was as sure he would not succeed. Richenda and Muller both had a look of contentment on their faces. They had accomplished what they had both set out to do. All unpleasantness would be buried along with those who had died today. All in all the future at the Muller estate looked bright.

The following months at Stapleford Hall would doubtless be unpleasant, but I consoled myself that I would at least see Merry again. I tried not to think of whether Rory would have returned to his post as butler. He had made it clear we no longer had a future together.

But so far my life had taken so many twists and turns I knew it was foolish to think anything was set in stone.

The publishers hope that this book has given you enjoyable reading. Large Print Books are especially designed to be as easy to see and hold as possible. If you wish a complete list of our books please ask at your local library or write directly to:

Magna Large Print Books
Magna House, Long Preston,
Skipton, North Yorkshire.
BD23 4ND

This Large Print Book for the partially sighted, who cannot read normal print, is published under the auspices of

THE ULVERSCROFT FOUNDATION